Praise for the Inspector DeKok Series by Baantjer

"Along with such peers as Ed McBain and Georges Simenon, [Baantjer] has created a long-running and uniformly engaging police series. They are smart, suspenseful, and better-crafted than most in the field."
—*Mystery Scene*

"Baantjer's laconic, rapid-fire storytelling has spun out a surprisingly complex web of mysteries."
—*Kirkus Reviews*

"DeKok is a careful, compassionate policeman in the tradition of Maigret; crime fans will enjoy this book."
—*Library Journal*

"DeKok's maverick personality certainly makes him a compassionate judge of other outsiders and an astute analyst of antisocial behavior."
—*The New York Times Book Review*

"It's easy to understand the appeal of Amsterdam police detective DeKok; he hides his intelligence behind a phlegmatic demeanor, like an old dog that lazes by the fireplace and only shows his teeth when the house is threatened."
—*The Los Angeles Times*

Inspector DeKok Series

Titles Available or Forthcoming from Speck Press

DeKok and
the Somber Nude

by
A. C. Baantjer

Translated by H. G. Smittenaar

speck press
golden

Published by *Speck Press,* speckpress.com
An imprint of Fulcrum Publishing
Printed and bound in the United States of America
ISBN13: 978-1-933108-16-2
Book layout and design by: Margaret McCullough, corvusdesignstudio.com

Library of Congress Cataloging-in-Publication Data
Baantjer, A. C.
[De Cock en het sombere naakt. English]
DeKok and the somber nude / by A.C. Baantjer ; translated by H.G. Smittenaar.
p. cm. -- (Inspector DeKok series ; no. 3)
ISBN 978-1-933108-11-7 (pbk.)
1. Crime--Netherlands--Fiction. 2. Amsterdam (Netherlands)--Fiction.
I. Smittenaar, H. G. II. Title.

PT5881.12.A2C6513 2007
839.3'1364--dc22

2007040955

10 9 8 7 6 5 4 3 2 1

1

_____

It was raining. It had been raining for days, endlessly long July days. Fat, heavy raindrops relentlessly pelted down from an even, grey sky.

DeKok felt vaguely melancholy. His mood was as sensitive as the most precise barometer; a long depression in the barometer found its counterpart in him.

With his big nose flattened against the window he surveyed the surroundings of the legendary police station on Warmoes Street. The rain veiled the nearby rooftops in a curtain of mist and water.

DeKok pressed his lips together. Deep creases appeared at the corners of his mouth. How often had he stood here lost in thought, grappling with crime and the underbelly of society. It had turned him into a grey old man: his upper body had acquired a distinct bow, his shoulders sagged. He thought about it not with bitterness but with his customary outlook of mild acceptance. Young Vledder, his assistant and fellow detective, came to join him at the window.

"A good thing," he said contentedly, "we have no important cases to investigate at the moment. I wouldn't look forward to going out in this weather. It's raining cats and dogs!"

"Well," nodded DeKok, "after all, we are in the middle of dog days." His broad, coarse face had the friendly look of a mild-mannered boxer. DeKok hesitated then said, "I remember my old mother. She didn't like this time of year. You see the old lady...she was a bit superstitious. She never failed to warn me: 'Careful, my boy,' she used to say, 'the dog days of summer can be dangerous.'"

He remained silent and scratched the back of his neck.

"Mother was right. In retrospect she was always right. She died during the dog days."

DeKok shoved his thick lower lip forward and looked up at the grey sky.

"I wouldn't want to die just now," he said after a while.

"What do you mean?" Vledder looked at him cautiously.

DeKok made a vaguely lazy gesture toward the heavy leaden sky. "The heavens are closed," he said somberly.

At that moment there was a knock on the door.

Both turned to face the door of the large detective room. There was a light on in the hall outside although it was the middle of the day. On the frosted glass of the door they observed the shadow of a hooded and cloaked figure. It was a picturesque if rather odd sight. Again there was a knock on the door.

"Enter," DeKok called out.

Slowly the opened and a young woman appeared in the door opening. She pushed her hood back and shook out her hair. DeKok estimated her to be in her early twenties. She was beautiful, he noted, extremely beautiful. Long blonde hair fell in waves over the collar of her black cape. She unhooked her wrap and pulled it with an elegant gesture from her slender shoulders. A small shower of fine raindrops cascaded to the floor around her. Vledder hastened to take her cape. She rewarded him with a faint, almost sad smile. Slowly she entered the detective room. As she progressed through the space the drab institutionalized room seemed to change from grey into a kaleidoscope of colors and sun.

With old-world charm DeKok offered her a chair next to his desk.

"Please sit down," he said in his most friendly manner.

"Thank you very much."

Carefully she sat down, placed her purse on the edge of the desk, and crossed her legs, a mesmerizing gesture. Her movements were slow, refined, and aimed at achieving a powerful impression.

DeKok looked at her resignedly. He quickly replaced enchantment with the cool observation of a trained detective. Her manner and movements no longer impressed him. He experienced the alluring scent of her perfume as attractive but nothing more. He sat down in the chair behind his desk.

"My name is DeKok," he said mildly. "DeKok with a kay-oh-kay." He waved in Vledder's direction. "This is my colleague Inspector Vledder, my right hand. How can we be of service?"

She did not answer at once, but hesitated as if not sure what to say. The hands in her lap moved in a cramped gesture. Her long, narrow fingers worried at the hem of her skirt.

"My name is Kristel van Daalen—van Daalen, with a double *A*."

DeKok smiled at her.

"You see, I'm very worried."

"Worried?"

"Yes, very." She sighed deeply.

"Why?"

She looked at him with big uneasy eyes.

"My cousin has suddenly disappeared."

"Disappeared?"

"Without a trace," she nodded emphatically.

"Since when?"

"Since yesterday, Mr. DeKok. Yesterday, Thursday, she left around three in the afternoon. I haven't seen her since. I went to look in her room when she didn't appear for breakfast and found her bed had not been slept in."

DeKok motioned to Vledder to make notes.

"What's your cousin's name?"

"Nanette, Nanette Bogaard." She paused, gave DeKok a faint smile, and added, "Bogaard, with a double *A*."

"Her age?"

"Nineteen. She would have been twenty next month, in August. We were born about two years apart."

The grey sleuth rubbed his hand over his chin, picking up on the young woman's use of past tense. Her manner of speaking affected him.

"Is it usual...I mean, does Nanette often stay out all night?"

"No. At least I don't think she did. You mustn't think that I watched her all the time. She went her own way. But the whole night away from home...that is a different matter. In any case I never, until now, missed her at breakfast. She was always in time to open the store."

"Store?" DeKok's eyebrows vibrated slightly.

"Yes, of course, Nanette and I own a flower shop along old Duke Street. You know, just off the Dam near the New Church, around the corner from Blue Street. I—we—live there, as well, upstairs and to the rear. Perhaps you know the store? Ye Three Roses?"

"I'm afraid," he answered slowly, "I'm only familiar with the bar The Three Bottles on Duke Street."

"I understand," she answered mildly. "The store isn't that old yet. Uncle Edward died less than two years ago. He liked us a lot, our Uncle Edward. He called us his daisies." She smiled almost shyly. "Nanette and I could always get along very well, you know, even as children. No quarrels..." She hesitated and then continued, "When Uncle Edward died he left us some money. Not a lot, but enough to start the business on Duke Street." She gestured vaguely around her. "We're both from Aalsmeer, daughters of growers. You know how that goes. You start to live and breathe flowers after a while. Our own flower shop in the middle of Amsterdam seemed ideal, like a dream. Uncle Edward's money made it possible to make a dream come true."

She silently removed invisible lint from her skirt.

"We complemented each other beautifully. Nanette was extremely gifted in an artistic way. The pieces she created were fantastic—little jewels. I don't believe that anybody in town did better arrangements. Because of the arrangements our store has gained some recognition. It was Nanette's doing."

DeKok looked at her searchingly.

"And what is your contribution to the enterprise?"

She smiled tiredly.

"I'm not artistic. I take care of the business end of the store. I have what Nanette called a 'bean-counter's soul.' Ach, I'm used to making ends meet; I grew up with it."

It sounded like an apology.

"And Nanette?"

"Nanette wasn't interested in money. She couldn't have cared less about it."

"What does interest her?"

She shrugged her shoulders in a careless gesture.

"Her passions were art and literature. All in all she was rather carefree."

The inspector nodded, understanding but still disturbed by her references to Nanette in the past tense.

"Perhaps, eh," he said hesitantly, "that's the explanation for her disappearance?"

She looked at him sharply.

"What do you mean?"

"Because of her carefree outlook there may be no reason to worry. Maybe she's just been held up by a friend and has just forgotten to give you a call?"

Nervously she pressed her hands together.

"It's really very nice of you," she sighed. "Really it's very nice that you're trying to allay my fears, but believe me, *something has happened to Nanette!* Something has happened to her. I'm certain."

"You're sure of that?" DeKok looked at her with some intensity.

"Yes."

"Why?"

"Call it female intuition, call it what you want. Laugh at my silly fears—it doesn't matter. I feel it in my bones." She remained silent as if at a loss for words.

Slowly DeKok rose from his chair and walked away from his desk. At some distance he stopped, turned, and looked at the young woman from behind. His sharp eyes, trained by years of experience, noted every reaction, even minuscule movements of her shoulders.

"Please go on," he said in a compelling voice. "Of what are you so certain?"

He saw her swallow.

"Nan—Nanette is dead," she stammered.

A strange silence came over the detective room after Kristel van Daalen's last words.

Vledder looked at DeKok with impatient, questioning eyes. He was not happy with the conversation, and a number of unanswered questions burned in his brain. DeKok understood his young colleague—he could see the impetuous youth within—and motioned for him to go ahead.

Vledder approached the shrinking figure in the chair purposefully. He seated himself importantly behind DeKok's desk and cleared his throat with a decisive sound.

DeKok watched from a distance. He liked his younger colleague, and he hoped Vledder would become his successor when he finally retired.

"Nanette is dead?" he heard Vledder ask. "At least that's what you say."

Kristel nodded.

"Yes," she said tonelessly, "Nanette is dead."

"A rather hasty conclusion, if you ask me." His voice sounded hard and penetrating. "There isn't a single clue to point in that direction. That is, you haven't mentioned a single reason for your suspicion."

The young woman raised tearful eyes toward Vledder, a determined expression on her face.

"If you want proof I can't give it to you. I'm sorry. I mean, I think I have been clear enough. It's just my feeling that Nanette is dead." She paused and took a deep breath. "And that is all. It should be enough for you." Her voice sounded reproachful, almost chastising.

Vledder's face became red.

"Feelings, feelings," he said loudly, "what use are those?"

DeKok interrupted soothingly.

"But they really are everything, aren't they, Miss van Daalen? Feelings are the basis of our existence."

She gave him a grateful look.

"But you must understand," he continued calmly, "that we need more information about your cousin. If we're to achieve anything at all we'll need some sort of starting point, some idea as to where and how to start our investigations. That's what my colleague meant to say. For instance, where was Nanette going yesterday?"

Kristel shrugged her shoulders. "I don't know," she said.

"Did she take a suitcase or an overnight bag?"

"No, I saw only her purse, nothing else."

"How was she dressed?"

"She had on a casual outfit, a blue suit."

"Did Nanette have friends?"

"You mean men with whom she associated?"

"Yes."

She made an expansive gesture.

"There were quite a few. Nanette had lots of friends. But recently she concentrated mainly on Barry Wielen, a journalist. He seemed nice enough, just a little fast...too fast for my taste."

DeKok grinned, turning on his charm.

"Journalists live their professional lives at top speed; it becomes ingrained. Have you talked to him about Nanette's disappearance?"

"No, I haven't talked about it with anyone. I came straight here."

"All right, leave everything to us from now on."

He scratched the back of his neck.

"Oh, yes," he added, "before I forget, do you have a picture of Nanette?"

She opened her purse. After a little searching she found a picture. It was a good clear image, roughly postcard size.

"It was taken about a month ago," she said.

DeKok took the picture from her and studied it with care. Nanette Bogaard was a beautiful girl, he noted. She looked a little like her cousin. The long blonde hair was the same, as was the structure of the face. She was perhaps a little slimmer, more fragile. He handed the photo to Vledder.

"You can go home now." DeKok placed a fatherly hand on her shoulder. "As soon as we know something we'll come and tell you at once."

He walked over to the peg and took her cape.

Slowly the girl rose from her chair. DeKok draped the cape over her shoulders.

"If you find Nanette at home, please let us know."

"No, Mr. DeKok, Nanette is dead."

She shook her head sadly.

2

DeKok paced up and down the detective room with his hands in his pockets. He mulled over the conversation with Kristel—the words, the intonations, the gestures.

DeKok could do that. He had a photographic memory and a love for detail. A seemingly unimportant slip of the tongue, a facial expression, he noticed it all. He was born with the gift, but his profession had honed his gift to a fine art.

He halted in front of the window, his favorite spot. It was still raining. Suddenly he turned around and walked over to the peg on the wall.

"Get your coat."

Vledder looked surprised.

"Say," he called with suspicion in his voice, "you're not planning to start looking for Nanette, eh…?"

"Bogaard," completed DeKok.

"Right, Bogaard. You're not already looking for her, are you? The girl has barely been gone twenty-four hours. Surely there's no reason to panic."

"Her cousin says she's dead." DeKok looked at him evenly.

"Her cousin is crazy. She's going off nothing but her feelings, female intuition. Just because this flower girl took it into her head to imagine her cousin dead you want to alert the entire police force?"

DeKok struggled into his old raincoat.

"No," he answered calmly, "not the entire police force, just the two of us. For the moment that ought to be enough."

Vledder shook his head in desperation. He couldn't understand the man. He walked over to DeKok, placing himself in front of the old sleuth, and raised a finger in the air.

"Just listen to me," he said, irritated. "Young Nanette has never been away from home, overnight, that is, according to her cousin."

"And?"

"And she's nineteen years old. DeKok, think: *nineteen*! This is just the age to start experiencing the occasional nightly adventure. What harm can it do? It's healthy."

"I know a lot of fathers," answered DeKok casually, "who would prefer some different sort of healthy activity for their nineteen-year-old daughters."

Vledder sighed.

"You know quite well what I mean. There's no question of a real missing person. What does Miss van Daalen want from us? She can hardly expect us to call out the troops every time a nineteen-year-old stays out all night. That's…" Vledder searched for the right word. "How can I put it? That's, eh, monks' work!"

"Come again?"

"Yes, you know, one letter at a time, year after year, never an end, you know what I mean."

DeKok laughed loudly. He placed his old, dilapidated

felt hat on the back of his head and walked out of the room. Vledder, furious, followed, his raincoat bunched up on his shoulders.

Barry Wielen was a tall, slender young man with friendly eyes and an old-fashioned moustache with points aiming proudly at the sky. DeKok was visibly impressed with the moustache; he looked at it with admiring attention. Wielen found this attention embarrassing. He moved restlessly under the searching eyes of DeKok.

"What do you want?"

The inspector shoved his hat a little farther on the back of his head and wiped the rain off his face with a handkerchief.

"That you take these wet raincoats from us."

The young man grinned, embarrassed.

"Of course, of course, I'm sorry."

Suddenly he came closer, helped remove their coats, put the coats away, and led the inspectors to a spacious room. It was somewhat cluttered but clean and cozy.

DeKok cleared off an easy chair and, without waiting for an invitation, sat down and stretched his legs with a groan of pleasure. Vledder followed his example. Wielen watched the performance with a surprised look on his face, a loss for words.

"What can I do for you, gentlemen?" It sounded a bit timid.

DeKok shaped his face into a friendly grin. It always surprised Vledder how attractive that made him look.

DeKok looked at Wielen from the depths of his easy chair and said, "Nanette Bogaard."

"Excuse me?"

"Nanette Bogaard," repeated DeKok. "She's still a minor, and we're here to collect her."

"I don't know what you're talking about," said Wielen, a vacant look on his face.

"It's really not all that difficult to understand," said the inspector. "We're inspectors attached to Warmoes Street station. We're looking for Nanette Bogaard, and according to our information, she's here with you."

"What?" a befuddled Wielen uttered again.

"Your vocabulary is rather limited. You also seem to be rather slow in the comprehension department... unfortunate traits for a journalist, I'd say. But all right, I'll try to be clearer: Nanette Bogaard, as stated, is an underage girl. We have reason to believe she spent last night with you. In the event you do not turn her over to us, or if you refuse to cooperate in our investigation, you may be charged with kidnapping." He paused for the desired effect then continued. "Kidnapping is, of course, a criminal offense." DeKok made it sound like a special treat.

The journalist looked at him, a dazed look on his face.

"You think I've committed a criminal offense?" he repeated.

"Yes, absolutely. Article 281 of our very own criminal code defines kidnapping. It is an interesting article. You should read it sometime. The minimum is six years with no parole."

"Six years?" Wielen looked anxious.

"Yes, a long time. When you finish, you'll be about thirty," nodded DeKok. He added, "But the maximum is life imprisonment, again without parole. You could very well die in jail."

Barry Wielen sat down and rubbed his hand over his eyes. He was trying to gather his thoughts. Normally he was able to control himself, able to control most any situation. It was something his profession required. But DeKok had given him no time.

He looked into the friendly eyes of the old detective across from him. His face appeared to be both cunning and irresistible. Slowly Barry got ahold of himself. The journalist in him took charge of the situation and decided not to knuckle under. A faint smile appeared underneath his gorgeous moustache.

"I wish it were true," he said.

DeKok looked at him, noting the change in attitude, and asked, "What do you mean?"

"I wish Nanette *had* spent the night with me. I must say, it is an exciting thought."

He grinned softly. His face became almost as attractive as DeKok's when he grinned.

"But I'm sorry to have to disappoint you," Wielen continued. "Nanette isn't here. She hasn't been here. Search the premises if you want. You'll not find her. I haven't seen her for at least two weeks."

"So you do know her?"

"Yes, of course. Nanette, wow-wow-wow, what a beauty...a treasure!" His entire face lit up. "The wild daisy from Ye Three Roses."

DeKok pulled up the left side of his mouth. It looked like a snarl.

"Wow-wow-wow?" he repeated evenly. "And when," he continued, "was the last time you saw Nanette?"

"I told you, about two weeks ago. It was more or less an accidental meeting."

"How do you mean 'more or less accidental'?"

"Well, eh—" suddenly he stopped. Wielen looked at DeKok. He looked from DeKok to Vledder and back again. A look of utter surprise came over him.

"Something is wrong here." He shook his head and then asked, "Why would two inspectors from Warmoes Street be interested in vice? You're homicide! Why this interest in Nanette?"

"She's gone."

"What do you mean *gone*?"

"Nanette is missing. Kristel van Daalen, her cousin, reported her missing this morning. Now do you understand our interest?"

Wielen nodded vaguely.

"Sure, sure," he responded, sounding distracted. Apparently he had some trouble accepting the disappearance of Nanette as fact. "Please go on."

"You spoke of an accidental meeting?"

Wielen leaned forward and reached for a pack of cigarettes on the coffee table. DeKok looked at the long, sinewy fingers of the journalist. They shook.

"Yes, yes, we met."

He lit the cigarette and inhaled deeply.

"It was evening. Around half-past ten, I think. I'd just left the paper after finishing up the report of a court case

I was assigned to earlier that day. I drove via the Dam
and skirted the Red Light District." He gestured with
his cigarette. "Suddenly I saw Nanette turn onto High
Street, she came from the Quarter."

DeKok looked incredulous.

"Nanette came from the Red Light District?"

"Yes, I too thought it strange. Really. I didn't know
her all that well, but Nanette never struck me as the kind
of girl who could be found anywhere near that part of
town. I could hardly believe my eyes."

"What did you do?"

"At first I drove on, then I turned and passed her from
behind. I looked in my rearview mirror."

"And?"

"I hadn't been mistaken. It was Nanette. I drove on
and parked on the Dam, near the monument. From there
I walked to Duke Street. I waited for her near Ye Three
Roses. It didn't take long. She arrived shortly thereafter."

"What did she say?"

Again Barry pulled on his cigarette.

"I just acted as if I'd met her by chance. I didn't
mention seeing her in the District. I didn't really dare
mention the subject. You understand, I didn't want to
give the impression that I'd been spying on her. After all,
I didn't have any right to call her on it."

DeKok looked at him searchingly then questioned, "I
thought that, eh, the two of you..."

A sad grin spread fleetingly over the face of the
young man.

"Ach," he said, "it's really never been more than a
slight flirtation, a game to Nanette."

DeKok listened to the tone of his voice.

"You're in love with her?"

Again Wielen sighed.

"In love, yes, you could call it that."

"Nanette hasn't reciprocated?"

Nonchalantly he shrugged his shoulders.

"She is too playful, not serious enough." He looked at DeKok for a moment. "After all," he concluded, "love is serious business, don't you agree?"

"Without a doubt," nodded the inspector. "There have been quite a few murders because of love. Certainly love is serious enough."

"Murders?" Wielen looked trapped.

"Love is one of the prime reasons for murder."

The journalist brought a hand up to his forehead. The intelligent look in his eyes disappeared. He started to grin like a fool.

"I, eh, I haven't killed Nanette," he almost stuttered.

DeKok reacted quickly. "Who said you did?"

"Nobody, nobody, but I thought, I mean..."

For a long time DeKok looked at Wielen thoughtfully. He rubbed his hand through his grey hair. He had weighed the reactions of the journalist, but his impressions were mixed. "Did Nanette say anything?" he asked.

"When?"

"That night, in front of her flower shop?"

"No, nothing. Well, I mean, we chatted a while. But she didn't tell me where she'd been that night. She went inside after about half an hour."

"And were you able to solve the puzzle later? I take

it the question of Nanette in the Red Light District worried you?"

"Indeed, but I haven't seen her since."

"So that was two weeks ago?"

"Yes, two weeks."

They remained silent together for a long time. The journalist lit another cigarette. He had barely finished the previous one. Young Wielen was obviously nervous, his tension well on display. There was a hunted look in his eyes and he was jumpy like a scared animal. His left hand kept turning the points of his extravagant moustache.

Vledder had at first listened carefully to the conversation between his colleague and the journalist, dutifully taking notes. And although he was more or less familiar with DeKok's methods, he always enjoyed seeing the master in action. But now his interest was waning. Vledder did not believe Nanette had disappeared. As far as he was concerned the girl had simply stayed out all night. No big deal. He thought DeKok was making too much fuss over the matter. Before long Nanette would reappear, and all this trouble would be for nothing. The thought made him highly annoyed. They had better things to do than run after a girl with a yen for adventure—in the pouring rain, no doubt.

Slowly DeKok looked around the room. His glance separated the clutter and took in the bare walls, absorbed the spare furniture. He stood up almost lazily, with slow movements.

The old inspector's trained eye had discovered something in Wielen's somewhat disordered room that was lovely, dissonant, sunny, and full of color. It had pride of place near the window, on top of a battered bookcase. There sat a small bunch of wildflowers artistically arranged in a thin, pale porcelain vase decorated with pink ribbon. A small masterpiece in the art of flower arrangement. DeKok walked over to the bookcase and lifted the vase in his hand. He looked at the flowers with interest. "Gorgeous," he murmured appreciatively, "extremely well done. I have seldom seen anything as fine as this."

After a while he replaced the vase carefully. It was as if he was handling a fragile religious relic. He stood and looked at it for a while longer, his hand supporting his chin.

"It's a pity," he sighed, "wildflowers are so fragile. They don't last long." His voice sounded genuinely depressed.

"It should be a crime. I mean, people should be prohibited from picking wildflowers. They belong outside in the fields, the woods, the streambeds."

He gestured at Vledder. "How long do you think these wildflowers will last, fresh and vibrant, in a stuffy bachelor's room?"

Carelessly Vledder shrugged his shoulders. He did not understand the direction, or the purpose, of DeKok's question.

"I don't know," he said hesitantly, "a few days...a week perhaps?"

DeKok nodded thoughtfully.

"A few days, a week," he repeated. "You're right. Certainly after a few days the slender stems would wilt."

Again he looked at the colorful bouquet, an admiring look in his eyes. Only after several minutes did he turn away. His face was expressionless, like a mask. He crossed the room and halted in front of the journalist.

"Barry Wielen," he said calmly, "there's but a single person able to arrange ordinary wildflowers in such a refined and artistic manner...your friend Nanette, the wild daisy from Ye Three Roses."

3

Inspector DeKok raked his thick fingers through his stiff, grey hair. It was a habit when he was deep in thought. Lazily he leaned back in his chair, his relatively short legs on the edge of the desk. Nanette's disappearance disturbed him, but he did not know exactly why. People disappear daily. Tracing them is one of the routine jobs assigned to detectives all over the country. Sometimes people who disappear are just plain tired—tired of their wives, their husbands. They have had it with jobs, bosses, houses, offices, and worries. In fight-or-flight mode people walk away from it all. But usually these flights toward freedom do not last long. It seems freedom too has its negative aspects. There is a certain comfort and protection in familiar surroundings, even in the sweet slumber of the daily grind.

DeKok pressed his lips together.

But Nanette, so it seemed, was different. There was no question of dissatisfaction with life, no flight from the daily grind. Something else caused her sudden disappearance, a different motive...but what?

Without more definite information there were no logical conclusions to be drawn, no matter how hard one tried.

He took his legs off the desk and produced a large sheet of paper from a drawer.

HOW OR WHY OR THROUGH WHOM DID NANETTE DISAPPEAR? he wrote in big letters at the top of the page. It was as if the thought so occupied him that he needed to see it in front of him as a sort of challenge to his imagination. He sighed, put the pen down, and looked at the question. Perhaps fear?

Vledder sat at his own desk, looking over his notes. He still did not understand DeKok's interest in the disappearance of Nanette Bogaard. It was commonplace to wait a few days before investigating reports of missing persons. That was the usual procedure. Long years of experience had shown it was virtually useless to panic right away when a person turned up missing. DeKok should know that. He was an old campaigner. How long had he been on the job—twenty, twenty-five years?

Vledder rose from behind his desk and walked toward DeKok. Despite everything, he genuinely liked his old mentor. It was a deep affection that had its origins in loyalty and admiration.

"Wow-wow-wow," he laughed.

Annoyed, DeKok looked up.

"Wow-wow-wow," repeated Vledder.

DeKok grinned disdainfully.

"It's a constant marvel to me," he said, "that the clear sounds of our beautiful language are constantly being improved." He snorted. "Heaven knows what the exact meaning of that primitive utterance may be."

Vledder laughed.

"Well you see, when a stallion spots a good-looking filly it starts to neigh—"

"I understand," answered DeKok. His tone was disapproving. "And when a civilized young man spots a beautiful girl he too reveals his feelings by uttering animal sounds."

"That's it!" Vledder remained silent for a while then continued. "But even without the strange 'wow-wow-wow,' I was amused immensely by the man. Wielen was as slippery as an eel. He knew what you were getting at with your commentary on wildflowers. He also knew that you had not one iota of proof."

Nonchalantly DeKok shrugged his shoulders.

"But our friend is lying all the same. Of course there's no legal evidence, I mean nothing you could take to court, but it was an indication to me that Wielen had seen Nanette at Ye Three Roses more recently than two weeks ago."

"How long do you think?"

"That arrangement couldn't have been put together long, maybe a day or so ago."

Vledder nodded then said, "But perhaps he's been in the shop but didn't see Nanette?"

"Of course that's possible. But I have the feeling Wielen is hiding something. He knows more than he's telling us."

Vledder grabbed a chair and sat down on it backwards, his arms folded on the backrest.

"What do you think? Should we have him followed?"

"Waste of time." DeKok shook his head. "That's hardly necessary with a reporter."

A look of consternation moved briefly across Vledder's face. "Not necessary? But if he—"

"Take it from me," interrupted DeKok, "the press boys are never very clever or cunning. They're merely bold and ill-advised."

He grimaced.

"Our old commissaris always used to say, 'Give a reporter enough rope and sooner or later he'll hang himself.'" There was nostalgia in DeKok's voice. "After all," he continued, "it's in the very character of a reporter. They can't fight it. Give them time and before long they'll publicize anything."

"Even their confession?"

"Perhaps," said DeKok, grinning. "It all depends on the size of the headline they think they'll get."

Vledder laughed.

"What about our boy's story about the District? Do you really believe he saw Nanette coming from there?"

DeKok scratched the back of his neck.

"I don't know," he hesitated. "He was rather glib with that story. He didn't need any prompting. That surprised me a bit, you know? I wonder if it could be a trap."

"Why do you say a trap?"

"Perhaps Wielen wants us to look for the cause of Nanette's disappearance in the District while—"

"The District has nothing to do with her disappearance," completed Vledder. Then he grinned and added, "The pimps and whores are as innocent as cherubs."

DeKok nodded approval while managing to show disapproval for Vledder's choice of words.

"But then," continued Vledder, "Wielen may be more cunning than you're trying to make me believe."

DeKok smiled faintly. He placed both hands on the desk and pressed his heavy upper body into a standing position.

"I've a little job for you," he said.

Vledder's eyes sparkled.

"You want me to track the reporter after all?"

"Just leave Wielen be. He can wait. I want you to go to Aalsmeer. Just ask around at the post there and have a little chat with Nanette's parents."

"You want me to tell them she's…"

"No, not yet. Just try to find out if the relationship between the two cousins is really as idyllic as Kristel led us to believe. Perhaps they know more about it in Aalsmeer."

Vledder nodded. His face was serious.

"And what are you going to do?" he asked.

"I'm going to see Lowee."

DeKok grinned broadly.

Lowee was better known in the Red Light District as "Little Lowee," for obvious reasons. He had a small body, a narrow chest, and a mouse-like face. Lowee and DeKok had known each other for years and had developed a mutual respect. Still, a barrier remained intact between them, a nebulous veil of wariness due to the fact that DeKok was a man of the law and Lowee a man of the underworld.

Lowee's intimate bar was near Warmoes Street, on the edge of the District by the corner of Barn Alley. The bar, with its shadowy interior, was the meeting place for the girls of the Quarter. This is where they rested, the likes of Black Tracy and Blonde Greta, sipping their sweet concoctions and chatting openly about the business.

DeKok shuffled to the end of the bar and hoisted himself onto a barstool. It was his regular place. From this vantage point he could look over the entire room.

Little Lowee came over to DeKok's spot at the bar and placed a glass in front of the detective. His other hand felt under the bar for the bottle of Napoleon cognac, which he never wasted on his regular customers. As a gesture of respect he reserved this delightful elixir exclusively for DeKok.

"How's crime?" asked Lowee pleasantly while he poured generously.

"Everybody has a cross to bear," grimaced DeKok. "My cross is the sins of others."

Lowee smiled with a crooked mouth.

"If I dint know youse better," he jeered, "I'd be weepin' in da drinks." He poured a generous measure for himself from the same bottle, raising his glass to DeKok.

"Proost to all dem kids of thirsty daddies."

DeKok grinned. "Proost!" he answered.

He rocked the glass slightly in his hand and inhaled the tantalizing aroma of the cognac. DeKok was a connoisseur. He took another small sip and enjoyed the sensation of inner warmth the liquor spread through his body. It banished the wet chill of the rain. Carefully he replaced the snifter on the bar.

"I'm looking for a girl."

Half surprised, Lowee looked at him.

"Youse…I'd have thunk youse done be far past it by now," he smirked.

DeKok ignored the remark. He took Nanette's picture from an inside pocket and placed it in front of the bar owner.

"This is the one."

Lowee wiped his hands on the front of his shirt and picked up the photo. He looked at it with care.

"Good-lookin' broad," he said finally, admiration in his voice. He pressed his lower lip forward, nodded his head emphatically, and repeated, "Yessah, very good-lookin' broad."

DeKok nodded agreement.

"Do you know her?" he asked.

He did not answer at once. He wiped the back of his hand over his mouth.

"She inda business then?"

DeKok shrugged his shoulders.

"To be honest, I don't know. She seems like a nice girl. Someone has asserted that she visits the neighborhood from time to time. But if you ask me, she doesn't belong."

"There's lotsa broads don't belong 'ere," snorted Lowee.

DeKok was aware of the correction. Little Lowee was rather touchy on that subject, as were most of the people who made a living from the underbelly of society. They didn't like "nice" people. As they often knew so well, nice was just a facade, a camouflage to hide behind. They saw too many so-called nice, respectable people in the District. They were not all tourists.

"I know what you mean," sighed DeKok.

Lowee sipped his cognac.

"Wassa she dun?" he asked casually.

DeKok smiled.

"No, no, it isn't that. The girl is gone, just gone. She disappeared without a trace. She's underage. A family member reported her missing."

Lowee's small, lively face cleared up. The subject of a disappeared underage girl was a safe subject in the neighborhood. It could freely be discussed with the police. The Quarter was not supposed to be a haven for underage runaways; that was the unwritten code of the Red Light District.

"How oldes we talkin'?"

"Nineteen."

"And youse gotta find 'er?" sniggered Lowee.

"What do you expect? It's my job."

"So and wadda we call dis flower?"

"Nanette, Nanette Bogaard."

"What youse say?"

"Nanette Bogaard."

The barkeep put his glass down and thought deeply. His face was distorted, as if in pain.

"Bogaard...Bogaard," he said thoughtfully, "I thinks I hear da moniker time or two."

DeKok sat up straight.

"Are you sure?" His voice was hopeful.

Lowee nodded vaguely.

"I woulda been very wrong if I'da sez otherwise." His lower lip curled itself upward. "Bogaard, youse see, itsa...a strange name around 'ere, youse remembers that."

With difficulty DeKok controlled his impatience.

"Where did you hear the name?"

"Musta bin right here, inna bar."

"A working girl?"

Lowee shook his head.

"Nope, notta broad, a guy."

"A guy, what sort of guy?"

Little Lowee pulled a face, as if in disgust.

"Ach, youse know, one of dem dirty stargazers... capable of anythin'. He come around a bit."

"I'd like to meet him."

"Dat's possible, 'e ain't been around long." He looked at DeKok and grinned. "But I don't think he'd be dyin' to meets youse."

DeKok shrugged his shoulders and drained his glass.

"Still, I would like to talk to him."

Lowee poured again.

"About da broad?"

"Yes, I find the similarity of names a bit too coincidental. Perhaps he knows something."

The barkeeper nodded.

"It ain't gonna be easy to catch up wid 'im. He's a shy sorta guy, I bin told."

DeKok bestowed his sunniest smile upon the small man.

"Perhaps, maybe, if you gave him a little encouragement—"

"Encouragement?"

"Yes, you know, a friendly invitation for..." DeKok looked at his watch, "...let's say tonight at eight. Tell him to go to 48 Warmoes Street, room nine."

"Da barn?"

"Yes."

A petite black girl, rather provocatively dressed, emerged from between the leather curtains that separated the bar from the minuscule lobby. A young man with dark glasses and dirty blonde hair followed close behind. Little Lowee looked over his shoulder. Through the large mirror behind the bar he followed the couple with his eyes. They sat down at a small table in the back. When Lowee turned back to DeKok, a tic had developed near his left eye.

"I, eh, I'se rather not," he said hesitantly.

DeKok rubbed his face with his hand.

"And I thought we were friends." It sounded reproachful. "I mean, such a small service isn't too much to ask now, is it?"

Lowee heard the disappointment and squirmed. His face assumed the usual painful expression. Obviously he was on the horns of a dilemma. A drop of sweat emerged from under his sparse hair and rolled down his forehead. DeKok's stare was steadfast.

"Well, what's your answer?" he pressed. "Will you do it?"

Little Lowee leaned close to DeKok in a confidential gesture.

"Why," he whispered, "don' youse ask 'im yourself?"

DeKok's eyebrows raised.

"Myself?"

Almost imperceptibly Lowee nodded.

"He just got 'ere."

4

Cognac glass in hand, DeKok slid off the barstool. With his decrepit little hat shoved onto the back of his head, the old detective waddled through the pinkish twilight of Little Lowee's bar. He looked like a drunk in his fifties, imbued with the belief that the sole purpose of mankind was to be drunk, jolly, and cozy at all times. In the far corner he halted. The conversation between the couple stopped immediately. DeKok smiled his best smile and, without invitation, allowed himself to sit down on the vacant chair next to the girl. She moved away stiffly, as though he were infected.

DeKok placed his cognac glass in front of him. After carefully placing both elbows on the edge of the small table, he rested his head on the entwined fingers of his hands and stared at the young man in front of him. He took in his face with a sharp gaze. The dark glasses hid some of his features, but a slight vibration around the corners of his mouth betrayed the young man's displeasure with the scrutiny.

"Go away," he hissed between his teeth. "Nobody called you over here."

DeKok took a careful sip of his cognac and played with the glass in his hand.

"I often come without being called," he said in a sepulchral tone of voice. "I'm like death. There's an element of surprise."

The young man hesitated. The tone of voice was not that of a drunk. It confused him.

"Well, we don't wish to be disturbed," he explained. "You understand?"

DeKok nodded.

"I understand," he said with a friendly note in his voice. "Therefore I won't keep you long. But in case you're interested, my name is DeKok. DeKok with, eh, a kay-oh-kay. I'm an inspector assigned to Warmoes Street station, homicide." He paused then continued. "As part of my duties I'm involved in an investigation regarding the mysterious disappearance of Nanette Bogaard."

"Nanette?" The young man was visibly shocked.

DeKok nodded.

"Nanette Bogaard," he emphasized.

The young man swallowed; his Adam's apple moved up and down.

"Disappeared?" he asked.

"Yes, are you interested?" DeKok looked at him sharply.

The young man threw a hunted look in the direction of his black companion.

"Well yes, no…not interested, not really, actually," he stammered. He motioned vaguely and nervously and tried to force a smile without succeeding. "Actually it's not all that peculiar. I'm sure that girls disappear all the time."

Slowly DeKok rose.

"Yes," he answered somberly, "sometimes they disappear forever."

He pushed his chair back, preparatory to leaving. It was an awkward movement, and his legs suddenly weren't quite so steady. In that instant DeKok lost his balance. He fell diagonally across the table. The empty cognac glass was knocked over. A murmur traveled through the room. DeKok stayed where he was. When he finally moved again, his hand touched the man's dark glasses as if by accident. Momentarily DeKok could see the eyes hidden behind the opaque lenses. It was just a moment, but enough for DeKok to get a flash of insight. He laughed, a bit embarrassed, murmured an apology, and waddled outside.

The couple looked after him with mixed emotions.

Little Lowee grinned from behind the bar.

As soon as the brown leather-reinforced curtains of Lowee's bar closed behind him, DeKok cinched tight the belt of his raincoat, pulled up his coat collar, and shoved his hat a bit farther over his eyes. Slowly he walked away from the bar. It was still raining. Lost tourists draped in wrinkled plastic paraded along the windows of the District. It was a sad amusement. DeKok looked at the wet, curious faces. This was Amsterdam in July. Sightseeing boats, their windows fogged over, moved through the canals.

At the end of the canal he stopped, undecided. He thought about returning to the station to request a nationwide search for the missing girl. So far he had resisted the urge. He felt it would be a bit premature. But he was more and more convinced something serious had happened. He had felt it all along—almost from the moment Kristel had uttered the name of her cousin. He couldn't shake a strange feeling of disaster, death, mystery. He'd had uncanny premonitions many times in the past, usually accurate premonitions. There were a number of logical explanations for Nanette's disappearance, but going over them did nothing to alleviate his fears. They remained in his subconscious, irresistible, like malevolent phantoms.

A cold drop of rain slid down the bridge of his nose. It reminded him how unproductive it was to stand on the corner of a street, especially in the rain. He cursed himself. Before long the wet would creep into his bones and he would have another cold. He was much too susceptible to live in the Dutch climate. His indecision was in the process of killing all initiative. He had to do something.

Upon further deliberation, he decided to wait a little longer with an APB. There was still time for that. Perhaps young Vledder had discovered something in Aalsmeer, and this entire matter would take a totally different direction. One never knew. An investigation involving a lively young girl had built-in surprises. Lively? Suddenly an idea crossed his mind. *How* lively was Nanette Bogaard? Was it possible the lack of liveliness was the cause of her disappearance? Melancholy, sorrow…could she have committed suicide? DeKok pressed his wet hat a little deeper into his forehead and walked in the direction of Duke Street. Kristel van Daalen, he thought, had to know something more.

Ye Three Roses stood as an exclusive flower shop with an artistic interior, exotic flowers, and fantastic prices. DeKok's careful bureaucratic soul would never allow him to send flowers to his wife from this particular shop. It wasn't because he did not wish his wife to have the best of everything, but for a man like DeKok there are, after all, limits.

The ding-dong of the store bell had long since faded to silence before Kristel van Daalen appeared behind the flagstone counter. Her appearance coincided with the soft whispering of bamboo curtains. Giving her a thorough look, DeKok again felt the allure of her extraordinary beauty. She looked fetching in a light blue duster.

The young woman approached him with a friendly smile and offered her hand. Her long, almost sinewy fingers closed around his hand. DeKok was surprised at the unfeminine strength of her grip, which was so in contrast with the rest of her appearance.

"Well, Mr. DeKok," she asked, "have you found a trace of Nanette?" Her voice sounded gaily hopeful.

Sadly DeKok shook his head.

"No," he said apologetically, "I don't know a thing yet. Of course we're trying, you understand. But so far we've had very little luck."

She nodded thoughtfully.

DeKok removed his hat and unbuttoned his coat.

"Do you have any suggestions?"

"Not one."

She shrugged her shoulders in a helpless gesture.

DeKok pointed at the wet storefront.

"I could imagine," he said, "that this kind of weather might make somebody suddenly long for another land, a different climate, a southern location full of warmth and sun-drenched beaches."

She disciplined a rebellious lock of blonde hair with the back of her hand.

"Surely you don't think Nanette—"

"It's only a suggestion."

"Do you find it plausible?" Doubt shone in her eyes.

"Actually I am applying my own feelings, longings if you like, to the situation. Whenever I see the window of a travel agency, full of posters with white sand, blue water, and people laughing in the sun, it has a profound effect. I always have the urge to just walk away from it all just to be there." He grinned self-consciously. "But at my age you always think about the consequences of such a bold step. The consequences are always far too many."

"And if you were younger?" She looked at him with interest.

DeKok grinned.

"How young? Nanette's age?"

Kristel did not answer. She glanced away and looked at the electric clock on the wall. She stared at it without seeing anything for a while. It was three minutes to six.

"I'll close up for the day," she decided. "It's almost that time anyway. I don't expect any more customers." She gave him a friendly smile.

"Perhaps you'd like to come in for a while?" she asked.

"Yes," nodded DeKok, "I'd like to see her room."

"What would you gain by seeing her room?"

"Perhaps there are letters or other papers that can help give us a starting point. Some young women keep a diary."

She was visibly upset at the thought.

"People still keep diaries these days?"

DeKok nodded. His face was serious.

"Not so often anymore. But some still do. Dreamy girls, those with romantic inclinations, sometimes feel the need to entrust their intimate thoughts to the pages of a diary. Some consider it a sort of confession."

"Confession?"

"Yes, a written declaration. It's very interesting literature. Sometimes it reveals the most surprising thoughts and disclosures."

DeKok made a tired gesture. He continued, "Most women are secretive about these writings. I mean, they're not easy to find. They're sometimes hidden in the strangest places."

She wrinkled her nose and snorted audibly.

"Silly," she said. "Childish."

The irritated tone did not escape DeKok.

"You never kept a diary?" he asked.

It was a superfluous question, and DeKok knew it.

She looked at him with animosity.

"I never," her voice sounded irked, "had time for such foolishness."

"And Nanette?"

She walked to the front door.

"I don't know," she remarked in passing, "I never paid any attention."

Carefully she closed the door. Two bolts and a Yale lock. Then she shut off a number of hidden light sources. Suddenly it was dark in the store. All color had disappeared.

"Are you coming?" she asked.

She disappeared behind the counter and through the bamboo curtain. Almost reluctantly DeKok followed the scent of her perfume. The scent excited him for a moment, a very brief moment.

She led him to a short, narrow corridor. A few brass hooks were attached to one wall, serving as clothing hooks.

"You can hang your coat here," she said and disappeared.

DeKok found a place for his old, much-loved hat and took off his raincoat. He quickly moved his hand over the shoulders and back of his jacket. It felt wet. He cursed quietly to himself. His raincoat had soaked through again. It was his own fault. His wife had told him time and again to get rid of the old coat and buy a new one. But DeKok did not like new things. He was attached to this raincoat almost as much as he was to his hat.

An oval mirror in a frame of Scottish plaid hung next to the brass hooks. He bent forward and looked at his reflection in the mirror. It seemed to cheer him up. He always felt that his face was a bit ridiculous and could never comprehend why others took him seriously. After all, with such a face…. He smiled at himself, adjusted his tie, and walked toward the door of the room. He stopped short in the door opening. It was as if everything had become hazy. There seemed to be a fog in front of his eyes, a magical veil of whispering taffeta and lace.

He rubbed the back of his hands over his eyes and tried to focus. She stood in the middle of the room, smiling. She was alluring in a fitted dress. The garment left little to the imagination and served as a witness to her beauty.

DeKok took a deep breath and succeeded in dispelling the enchantment. He wondered how she'd tricked him, what had veiled his clear observation. He analyzed: It had been her smile, he decided, and her look full of sweet promise. It had been the cause of a slightly increased heartbeat and flow of blood to the head. Embarrassed, he scratched the back of his neck and banished his foolishness with a grin. Then he entered the room.

She motioned to a wide bench near the wall.

"Please sit down," she said warmly, making him feel at home. "I'll make some coffee." She disappeared into the kitchen.

DeKok sat down and looked around. The room was tastefully furnished. Old, new, antique, and modern balanced in a near perfect harmony. A spiral cast-iron stairway with teak treads had been cunningly made part of the interior. The room could not be imagined in any other way.

A small Swedish desk in one corner of the room displayed the picture of a girl in a nurse's uniform. The desk was shaded by an unlit floor lamp. DeKok could not make out the figure in the photo.

Kristel returned from the kitchen with a set of transparent glass balls and a complicated-looking contraption. Somewhere near the bottom a flame caused the coffee to percolate through the system. The smell was heavenly. With an elegant leg she pushed a small table closer, and then placed the contraption on it along with cups and other ingredients.

"Cream and sugar?"

DeKok nodded.

She sat down next to him and poured.

"I'm glad you came," she said softly, "it was quite a relief. You see, all day I've been dreading this hour. Nanette and I always drank coffee together around this time. It was sort of a ritual—close the shop, make coffee."

"I understand completely," nodded DeKok.

She stirred her cup.

"We only had each other. We were dependent on each other."

DeKok looked at her from the side.

"You don't have visitors?"

"We have no girlfriends."

"What about male visitors?"

A blush appeared on her cheeks.

"I have always categorically discouraged male visitors."

"Why?"

She sighed.

"I didn't want any loose talk in the neighborhood."

"This is Amsterdam, not Aalsmeer," grinned DeKok.

"You think this place is so different?" She looked at him sharply.

DeKok did not answer. Then he asked, "What does Nanette think?"

She took a hasty swallow of her coffee.

"Nanette? Nanette accepted it."

"So she doesn't agree?"

Her face became hard.

"She accepted it."

DeKok sighed.

"I wonder," he thought aloud, "what Nanette's reaction would be if she were to suddenly come in and see us together?"

Kristel turned her face toward the door. Her eyes were large and scared. "Nanette? No, that's impossible," she said.

She took DeKok by the arm.

She almost screamed, "That just couldn't be!" There was terror in her voice. "Mr. DeKok, please tell me it would be impossible for her to just come in unexpected without my noticing."

DeKok shook his head.

"Don't worry," he said calmly, "with two bolts on the front door that would be quite a trick."

His sarcasm escaped her.

"I'm afraid, Mr. DeKok."

He looked at her searchingly, trying to penetrate to the thoughts beyond the enchanting exterior.

"What, or whom, do you fear? Surely it's not Nanette. You think she's dead, correct?"

"Yes, yes, she's dead," she panted.

DeKok rubbed his face with his hand. This had come full circle—this was reminiscent of Vledder's heavy-handed interrogation earlier in the day when he dismissed Kristel's emotional state. But DeKok was looking for a calm interview, with time and opportunity for confidences. He doubted he would succeed, however. There was something wrong with Kristel van Daalen, something he did not understand. She seemed so...schizoid, so unstable. She would appear infinitely desirable and enchanting, then without warning she would change into a threatened madwoman. Was Nanette's disappearance the only reason for the mood swings?

He looked at the lovely woman next to him. Right here, he thought, but unattainable, enigmatic. He looked at her pale face. She was still overwrought. Calmly he drank his coffee and waited for her to calm herself.

"Could I see her room now?"

She rose and pointed at the spiral staircase.

"Just go upstairs and push the trapdoor at the top of the stairs, it's counterbalanced. I'll follow."

DeKok nodded. He did not know what he was looking for in Nanette's room, he just wanted to know what the room looked like, the color of the curtains, the fabric of her nightgown. DeKok felt that these things were important. They would help him to form a mental picture of the missing girl.

Upstairs Kristel showed him around.

In the back there was an additional workroom. Red earthenware flowerpots were spread all over the floor. The walls were covered with racks and shelves loaded with beads, glasswork, straw, and raffia in various lengths and sizes. It was a riot of colors. There were spools of green wire and plastic ribbons in many colors and widths. The air smelled of earth and rotting moss.

Nanette's room was a disappointment. It was a functional bedroom, without frills and sparsely furnished. A single bed without cover was set along one wall next to a small makeup table. There was an extensive collection of makeup articles schematically arranged. A large wardrobe stood against the opposite wall. DeKok opened the doors. To the left was quite a wardrobe of coats, suits, and dresses. To the right on shelves were sweaters, shirts, and a stack of underwear. The top pair was green. DeKok read the word "Thursday" in embroidered letters. He lifted it up and discovered a pink pair of underwear with "Friday," a sky blue set with "Saturday," and yellow ones with "Sunday."

Monday, Tuesday, and Wednesday were missing.

Softly DeKok closed the large chest doors. He looked around one more time and left the room. He had seen enough, and unfortunately there were no letters, personal papers, or a diary.

Kristel led the way along the corridor. Along the way she stopped in front of another door.

"And this is my room," she said.

DeKok looked at her. Her face had regained the warm expression of happy generosity. Her blue eyes mirrored a sea of promises.

"Would you like to see it?"

"Please."

Suddenly shy she slowly opened the door as if reluctant to reveal a part of herself, to reveal a secret. There was a comfortable aura of feminine intimacy about the room. It reminded him of the closeness of a boudoir from centuries past. In striking contrast the night table held a photo in a very modern frame. It showed an athletic girl in shorts carrying a tennis racket. She noticed DeKok's glance and smiled.

"That's history. I almost never play anymore."

"Why not?"

"No time. The business takes all my spare time."

DeKok nodded.

"Does Nanette practice any sports?" he asked. "Does she have any hobbies?"

She shook her head.

"No, Nanette was just beautiful."

DeKok looked at her searchingly. There was something in her voice that he did not like.

"Have you," he began with some hesitation, "eh, ever been in love?"

Annoyed, she looked at him.

"In love?"

"Yes, in love."

He noticed the blue in her eyes change to a steely grey. Her eyes flashed.

"What does that have to do with Nanette's disappearance?"

DeKok made a tired gesture.

"That's exactly what I'm wondering."

5

DeKok held a lonely vigil behind his desk in the deserted detective room. It was hot. The temperature resembled the oppressive heat inside a kiln. DeKok had lit one of the giant gas radiators near the window and draped his raincoat nearby. He was determined to dry it, along with his hat. He had promised himself dry clothes and, by Jove, he was going to have dry clothes. He was not going to leave the room until his immediate goals had been achieved—even if he received information that half the city had been murdered. Dry clothes first, next a long period of nothing, and then, only then, everything else. The annoyed look on his face was emphasized by a stubborn set to his jaw.

DeKok was not in good humor. The interview with Kristel van Daalen had not gone according to plan. He would have liked to have cracked that hard shell, but she kept evading him. As long as he remained under the influence of her physical beauty, as long as he seemed spellbound, she was all sweetness and light. Then he would struggle free of her captivating spell. Once he returned to asking questions, examining facts, she became manic. It was a strange situation. He thought, Kristel asks for help from the police regarding the disappearance of Cousin Nanette, but as soon as the police start to ask questions, the same Kristel clams up like an oyster.

He loosened the top button of his shirt and looked pensively at the heat shimmering above the radiator. He thought about withdrawing from the case. Just issue an APB and let the consequences be the consequences. If the interested parties were not going to cooperate, then why should he worry his head about it? After all, it was possible that Nanette had just taken off. "I have always categorically discouraged male visitors." He grinned to himself. Did Kristel really expect to keep love at bay with that attitude? It was rather silly. He took a blank text form and thought about what he wanted to write. After some deliberation he decided on a blanket APB, including the border posts.

He wrote: *The Commissaris of Police, Chief 2nd Division, Post Warmoes Street in Amsterdam, requests to be informed of the whereabouts of Nanette Bogaard, age nineteen. Description: Approximately 5 feet 6 inches, slender, long blonde hair with natural wave. Last seen dressed in a dark blue suit and—*

He put the pen down. Suddenly he remembered what he had seen in Nanette's room—the underwear with the days of the week. He pursed his lips together and shook his head. Something was out of place. According to Kristel, Nanette had disappeared yesterday, a Thursday. But the underwear with "Thursday" were still in the wardrobe. If Nanette really was in the habit—and it seemed she was—of wearing them in order according to the day of the week, Kristel had been lying. Nanette had *not* disappeared Thursday; she was already gone by Wednesday.

Suddenly DeKok began to laugh. He laughed loudly. It was high time that he took a long, sober look at Nanette's case. He was getting upset over nothing, starting to see suspects around every corner. Never mind the pondering over underwear. That was ridiculous, of course it was. After all, what woman was going to be dictated by the days written on a pair of underwear—one in a thousand? It was probably fewer. In that moment he could visualize himself in front of the judge: "And then, Your Honor, underwear in her closet, eh, ladies' garments, Your Honor, and...eh, embroidered thereupon..." The defense (and the press) would have a field day. The telephone on his desk started to ring. He lifted the receiver; it was Vledder.

"I'm back from Aalsmeer."

"All right. Where are you now?"

"At the post near the stadium. I just called to see if you were still there."

"Why?"

"Well, if you had gone home then I would have gone home as well. I have a date tonight, you see, with a girl."

"So?"

"Yes, well, but if you had planned anything for tonight, you see..."

"Have you known her for some time?"

"Who?"

"The girl."

"About three months."

DeKok thought for a while.

"Does she wear underwear with the days on them?"

"What!?"

"You know, panties with the days embroidered—one pair for each day of the week."

He heard Vledder sputter.

"It's never gone that...eh, I mean, eh, it's rather an intimate piece of apparel."

"Right, that's what this is all about. It was just a shot in the dark. Apparently the sexual revolution of today is less a reality than it would appear. You just keep your date."

There was silence on the line for a while.

"DeKok, are you going to be in the office much longer?"

"Oh, maybe another half hour or so."

"Okay, then I'll see you shortly."

"Why? Did you discover something important in Aalsmeer?"

"No, but you sound like you have a fever or something."

Vledder sounded worried.

"Go fly a kite!"

DeKok threw the phone down and used his handkerchief to wipe the sweat off his forehead. It was getting hotter in the room. He was just about ready to shut the radiator off when the phone rang again. This time it was the desk sergeant downstairs.

"Somebody down here's asking for Inspector DeKok, with a kay-oh-kay."

"What kind of somebody?"

"A young man about twenty-seven with—"

"Dark blonde hair and dark glasses," completed DeKok.

"Precisely."

"Is he alone?"

"Yes."

"Fine, just send him up, will you?"

DeKok replaced the receiver and hastened to turn the radiator off. He was starting to melt. His hands stuck to every surface he touched.

He took his coat from the hanger and opened the window for some fresh air. It had finally stopped raining, he noticed. From his vantage point he looked down on small groups of people in the street. It was busy in the streets. The bars across the street from the station generated noise. From somewhere a lone man sang a sad song: "Mother, I cannot live without you..." DeKok could relate. It sounded convincing, a real tearjerker. There was a knock on the door.

DeKok closed the window and walked back to his desk. He dried his face on his handkerchief once more, then draped his jacket over the back of his chair and rolled his shirtsleeves up. Only then did he call, "Enter!"

The door opened slowly and the young man whom he had first met in Lowee's bar entered with obvious reluctance.

DeKok smiled encouragingly and pointed at the chair next to his desk.

"Sit down, my friend," he said in a friendly tone of voice.

The young man's face revealed his antagonism.

"I'm not your friend."

DeKok grimaced.

"You're right," he admitted in a resigned sort of voice. "As far as friendship is concerned one cannot be selective enough. In any event, what can I do for you?"

The young man swallowed.

"What's the matter with Nanette?"

DeKok moved his eyebrows. Those who knew him well swore DeKok's eyebrows sometimes took on a life of their own. They could actually ripple. Vledder could stare at them for minutes at a time, mesmerized.

"I thought you weren't interested?" asked DeKok finally.

"I'm sorry but I am—interested, I mean."

DeKok sighed.

"But this afternoon—" he began.

"That was this afternoon," interrupted the irritated young man. "I could hardly show my concern in front of my lady companion. How would I explain my interest in the disappearance of another girl?"

"What's the problem? Pearl isn't the jealous type."

"Pearl?" the young man asked, surprised. "You know her?"

DeKok smiled.

"Black Pearl of Cuba, oh, yes. Sometimes when she's in a good mood she'll call herself the 'Jamaican Whirlwind' or the 'Caribbean Hurricane.'" He snorted depreciatingly. "Not that it means a whole lot, but for a virtually unknown singer in small bars it always sounds so much better than 'Black Mary from Rotterdam.'"

The young man stroked his hands along his lips.

"You, eh, you're well informed."

DeKok shrugged his shoulders.

"Ach," he said almost apologetically, "that doesn't mean a lot in the case of Pearl. Almost every guy in the neighborhood can tell you the same thing. It's really no secret. I think, Mr. Bogaard, Pearl's interested in you because you're relatively new to the neighborhood."

"What do you mean by new?"

Smiling, DeKok leaned closer.

"What are you hoping to find in the neighborhood, Mr. Bogaard?"

"Nothing. I live here, near the old sea dike."

"What are you hoping to find, I asked?"

"I…eh, I told you, I live here."

DeKok leaned even closer. His face almost touched the face of the young man next to his desk. He whispered.

"Mr. Bogaard, how long have you been sick?"

The young man started to laugh nervously.

"Sick? I'm not…"

DeKok nodded emphatically.

"Yes, I'm asking how long."

The young man became more and more agitated. DeKok did not miss any of it. The man's eyes moved restlessly behind the dark glasses. His hands, although pressed flat against his knees, shook.

"How long?" repeated DeKok in a compelling voice.

Bogaard did not answer.

Then, suddenly, after a few flashing movements, DeKok held him in a steel-like grip. Holding the young man's wrist with one hand he pushed a sleeve up with the other hand. It happened so fast, so totally unexpectedly, that even if the man had anticipated it he could not have prevented it. Accusingly the pale, naked inner arm of Bogaard was exposed in DeKok's grip. The tracks and puncture marks spoke their own clear language.

"Morphine?"

The young man nodded silently. His handsome face had a sad, almost painful expression. His lower lip quivered like a child who is about to burst into tears.

DeKok let go of the arm and felt pity.

"If I hurt you," he said, concerned, "I'm sorry. Such was not my intent. But I had to know about your malady. You understand, you're not the type one finds in this neighborhood. Therefore, I wondered…"

Bogaard pulled his sleeve down and adjusted his clothes.

"Happy now?" It sounded bitter.

DeKok looked at him suspiciously.

"Why should I be happy because you're sick with morphine? I should gloat over your affliction? What do you take me for, Mr. Bogaard, a sadist?"

"Perhaps."

DeKok did not react at once. Silently he looked at the young man for some time, a thoughtful expression on his face.

"Yes, perhaps," he said after a while. "But you cannot read my mind, just as I cannot read yours. We're all guilty of mouthing one sentiment at times while thinking the exact opposite." He made a wry gesture with his hands. "It's the cause of many a misunderstanding," he concluded.

At that moment Vledder entered the detective room in his usual exuberant way. He hung his coat on a peg and looked with surprise from DeKok to the young man and back again.

"You have a visitor?"

DeKok smiled.

"Let me introduce you to Mr. Bogaard."

Vledder tried to ripple his eyebrows in true DeKok style, but instead had to settle for wrinkling his forehead.

"Bogaard?" he asked.

The young man rose and shook hands with Vledder.

"My mother's name. I, eh, I write under that name."

"You write?" asked DeKok.

A bitter smile played around the lips of the young man.

"Ever heard of Frank Bogaard?"

Vledder's eyes glistened. He nodded emphatically.

"Of course, of course! I've read your books. *The Quiet End* and *The Transparent Death*. Each book caused rather a sensation some years back, especially among your young adult readership. It was a fairly dark future you predicted in your books, if I remember correctly. I devoured both books."

Bogaard sighed.

"Yes, most readers of the older generation have rejected my books. They find them too nihilistic." He grinned. "It is as if they were never brought up in the shadow of the A-bomb—as if it was something to cheer about."

DeKok had never read anything by Frank Bogaard, but he could imagine the tendencies of his books: life without hope, death without release. It did not seem appealing reading material.

"Bogaard, you said, is your mother's name?"

"Yes."

"So Nanette isn't your sister?"

"No, Nanette is my cousin."

"And when did you last see her?"

The young man pulled on his lower lip.

"About two weeks ago, I think."

"Where?"

"In my room here in the Quarter. She came to visit me. Since my mother's death, Nanette has been the only one in my family who still has anything to do with me."

"Why's that? Are you a black sheep?"

Frank smiled.

"You could say that. My lifestyle and ideas aren't exactly what you'd expect from someone with a middle-class background. And the van Daalen family is very middle class."

DeKok looked at him, his head cocked.

"Van Daalen with a double *A*?"

"Yes, my father was Martin van Daalen, a grower."

"And Kristel?"

"Kristel is my sister."

DeKok raked his hands through his hair. He had to absorb this information slowly. His glance fell on the face of the young man. There were some similarities, minute similarities. Frank van Daalen's face was more delineated, sharper. The signs of his addiction were easy to read. Opiate addiction had deepened the creases in his face. His skin tone was dull and sallow.

"Did she ever visit you?"

"Who, Kristel?"

"Yes."

The young man grinned without mirth.

"I don't think she even knows where I live. She certainly doesn't know I live in Amsterdam. You see, we've become estranged over the last few years." Reflecting, he looked past DeKok, apparently overcome by memories. Then he continued, "It used to be so different before. Yes, when we were younger we really liked each other."

"No longer?"

He shook his head sadly.

"Kristel," he said slowly, "has remained a van Daalen."

DeKok nodded his understanding.

"And you became a Bogaard?"

Frank lifted his glasses and rubbed his eyes with a tired gesture.

"Yes, I became a Bogaard."

They remained silent. After a while DeKok rose and walked to the small counter and the percolator. He felt like a cup of coffee. He filled the pot from the tap, put coffee in the top of the percolator, and placed the assembled unit on the flame. DeKok liked the old-fashioned percolator. He did not believe in the modern electric coffeemakers.

Vledder pushed his chair closer to young Bogaard.

"When," he asked, genuinely interested, "will you publish your next book?"

The face of the young man became even more somber.

"That, eh, that I don't know. That's difficult to say. You never know when inspiration will hit you. Sometimes it stays away for a long, long time. Could be gone forever."

DeKok, his back to the two men, seemed to detect a

tone of anxiety or fear. Slowly he turned toward them.

"What was your last book, Bogaard?"

The young man hesitated momentarily.

"*The Transparent Death*," he said with a sigh.

Vledder looked shocked.

"*The Transparent Death*?" he asked. "But that was quite some time ago, yes?"

"Yes, four years." He sounded dispirited. "I wrote *The Transparent Death* four years ago. It took less than three months to complete. I wrote day and night, like a man possessed. When I turned the manuscript in to the publisher I had a feeling of immense release. I had been freed from a demon. My publisher merely said, 'Give me another one.'"

He took off his dark glasses and hid his face in his hands.

"It became torture; stories haunted me. Suddenly I lost it. I was finished, written out. Never mind writer's block. Ha! Writer's disability was more like it. No matter what I tried my head was a vast, hollow space. There was absolutely nothing—no thoughts, no feelings, no content. I was so drained."

Suddenly he started to sob like a child. His body shook. He lifted his head. His large, wet eyes looked beseechingly at DeKok. His lips quivered and his hands stretched toward the grey sleuth.

"Where is Nanette?" he cried.

DeKok did not answer. Searchingly he looked at the young man. Without the dark glasses the similarity between him and Kristel was much more noticeable, especially the shape and color of the eyes.

"Where is Nanette?"

The young man's voice was close to hysteria.

"Where is Nanette?!" he screamed.

DeKok remained outwardly unmoved. He noticed how Bogaard's body started to shake convulsively. His mouth pulled in nervous tics. It was frightening, terrifying. His face lost all color; it became white as marble. Cold sweat appeared on his skin.

"*Nanette*!?" It sounded like a death knell.

Completely agitated he got out of the chair and started to wave his arms around. His movements resembled those of a man being pulled down into a maelstrom, trying to reach a life preserver he couldn't reach.

Vledder took hold of Bogaard from around the waist from behind and spoke to him forcefully, convincingly calm. Nothing helped. The young man continued to scream, out of his mind, foam showing on his lips.

"*Nanette*!!"

DeKok looked on from his place next to the percolator. He did not interfere. He knew it was useless, knew the episode would not last much longer.

Bogaard swayed suddenly, a grotesque movement without sense or volition. Then his muscles relaxed and his eyes glassed over. His head fell sideways. A deep sigh escaped from his chest, and his body slowly slid from Vledder's arms onto the floor.

6

The impassive paramedics did not say much. They placed the weak, exhausted body of Frank Bogaard on the stretcher, arranged a blanket over him, and tightened the broad leather straps. Then they carefully lifted the stretcher and carried it down the long corridor. They maneuvered it almost vertically down the tight staircase to the ground floor. The exercise went smoothly, routinely. It was a quiet demonstration of compassion.

DeKok walked down the stairs behind the stretcher.

The desk sergeant made a vague gesture toward the stretcher and raised his eyebrows.

"Hey, DeKok," he grinned, "what do I put in my report? Another victim of the *third degree*?"

DeKok did not appreciate the coarse humor.

"Just report it as a man who fell sick, probably due to slow poisoning as a result of substance abuse," he answered mildly.

The desk sergeant snorted.

"He looks overdue for his next fix, more likely," he remarked. He looked at the pale face on the stretcher and pushed his lower lip forward. "They say we should show compassion. I suppose so." It did not sound very convincing. "Where'd he come from anyway?"

"He reported to you a while ago, don't you remember? You sent him upstairs," answered DeKok.

The desk sergeant thought. A pained expression showed on his face.

"You're right," he admitted. "The pale one with the dark glasses. I rang you." He took a notepad and dictated to himself: "Man, under own volition, appeared at this post and left via ambulance of the city medical service to..."

He looked at the paramedics.

"Where are you taking him?"

They put the stretcher down.

"To 'Old Willy,'" answered the older one.

"Wilhelmina Hospital," wrote the sergeant.

"What do you think?" asked DeKok. "Are they going to keep him in the hospital or are they going to let him go as soon as he recovers?"

The older paramedic shook his head.

"They're going to keep him for observation, at least for a day or so. If it's really bad they'll keep him in detox. That's the usual procedure anyway."

"And then?"

"Just hope he doesn't start again. If he gets hold of even the smallest dose he'll be hooked again."

The second paramedic nodded agreement.

They picked up the stretcher once more and walked out of the station. The ambulance was backed up to the front door. A constable helped them load.

The smell of coffee greeted DeKok when he returned
to the detective room. Vledder had finished making the
coffee and prepared two mugs.

"Gone?"

DeKok sat down behind his desk. With both hands
around the mug he began to slurp his coffee. It was a
most unattractive sound. His thoughts were with Frank
Bogaard, his dependency on drugs and his wild desire
for his cousin. The cry of "Nanette" still resonated in his
ears and his brain.

"Is he gone?" repeated Vledder.

DeKok nodded.

"For the time being they're taking him to Wilhelmina
Hospital for observation. Perhaps they'll put him in for
drug rehab; that is, if he plans to cooperate. It's of course
the only cure."

Vledder sighed and then said, "Can you fathom it?
Such a talented, intelligent guy—you'd expect such a
man would know the inevitable results. If you persist you
fall into a kind of hell; everybody knows that."

DeKok replaced his mug on the desk.

"If you persist..." he repeated slowly.

"What do you mean?"

"No more than what I said. You see, nobody plans
to become enslaved. People expect to escape getting
hooked. Every user thinks he or she is the exception: 'I
can quit whenever I want.' It starts with a small dose, just
a remedy, really. Maybe it will help with a temporary
physical pain or maybe a mental issue...or even writer's
block."

Vledder looked surprised.

"You seriously believe that's why Bogaard started taking drugs?"

DeKok shrugged his shoulders.

"I don't know. Perhaps, though. We really don't know enough about our friend to come to any definitive conclusion. In any case, he's been hooked for some time. Judging by his physical deterioration I would guess at least a year, perhaps longer. The best thing is to check with the doctor tomorrow. Meanwhile we have a very important question to answer."

"Question?"

DeKok nodded.

"Yes, how does Frank Bogaard get the stuff? Who do you think is his supplier?"

Carelessly Vledder shrugged his shoulders.

"He lives in the Quarter, right? Considering the area, there are plenty of contacts. Maybe he moved into the Quarter in order to be closer to his source. Otherwise what could he possibly be looking for there?"

DeKok did not answer at once. He had a very annoying habit of ignoring things when he wanted to do so. This time, however, it was inadvertent. Hands under his chin, both elbows firmly on the edge of the desk, he looked thoughtfully at nothing in particular. A sudden thought occupied his mind.

"You know," he said suddenly, "addiction can cause people to do the strangest things. Even the meekest may be moved to violent acts. When they're unable to get a fix or if their drug is withheld, they're liable to do anything…even murder."

Amazed, Vledder looked at DeKok.

"You're not thinking that Frank Bog..." he did not finish the sentence.

"What?"

"You don't think Frank Bogaard had anything to do with Nanette's disappearance?"

"What's so strange about that?"

"Nothing, I mean, but..."

DeKok stood up from his chair and started to pace across the dusty floor of the detective room. He could arrange his thoughts better to the beat of his shuffling gait.

"What did Frank Bogaard do?" he asked in the tone of a professor in front of his students. "What did he do when he became uncomfortable just now?"

Almost mechanically Vledder answered, "He went into convulsions and started to cry out."

"Exactly, he started to cry out. For whom did he cry out? Nanette. Why?"

Vledder shrugged his shoulders.

"He wanted her, eh, he needed her."

"What for?"

"I don't know."

DeKok halted in front of Vledder.

"All right, taking into account his addiction, what did Frank need more than anything at that time?"

"His next fix."

DeKok nodded approvingly.

"Exactly. And whose name did he keep shouting?"

"Nanette's!"

Suddenly there was a gleam in young Vledder's eyes.

"Of course," he exclaimed, "he called Nanette but meant *morphine*!"

DeKok raised an index finger in a most pedantic manner.

"And what does that mean?" he asked.

"That means," answered Vledder, suddenly very serious, "that in Frank's mind the notions of morphine and Nanette are closely interrelated. There is really almost no difference."

DeKok let himself down in his chair.

"In other words, Nanette is his supplier."

Sighing, Vledder shook his head.

"It was right in front of me," he said, still shocked by the quick succession of startling thoughts. "Nanette Bogaard, the wild daisy from Ye Three Roses, is also a drug dealer."

"Whoa there, my young friend, don't go overboard. She supplies Frank, or at least used to. Of that I'm almost certain. But it is premature to suspect her of being a dealer in the sense you describe. We cannot conclude that."

Vledder grinned.

"Premature? First of all we can safely assume that Frank pays dearly for his pleasures. We're not going to assume, I hope, that Nanette delivers free of charge?"

DeKok pulled on his lower lip and let it plop back. He repeated the gesture. It made a most annoying sound.

"Free of charge? No, street prices are pretty hefty. But I don't think that Nanette is in it for the money. You remember what Kristel told us? Nanette isn't interested in money, she couldn't care less."

"Yes, yes," exclaimed Vledder, animated, "that's what Kristel said. But how far can we trust her? Perhaps that entire flower shop is no more than a front for drug trafficking."

DeKok laughed heartily.

"Oh, yes, for sure," he mocked. "I can see it now: a field full of poppies at the ancestral homesite in Aalsmeer, and an opium distillery from The Three Bottles down the street."

Vledder pulled a face, discouraged by DeKok's cynical tone.

"Well yes, if you put it that way," he said almost shyly. "It was only a theory, you know."

DeKok grinned. His old, craggy face looked almost boyish.

"Well don't let it get you down. I was only joking. You're right, the flower shop could be an ideal front. But I don't believe it is. No, I don't believe it at all. It requires a completely different setup and different characters—more cunning, calculating, and callous. I went to Ye Three Roses this afternoon and had Kristel show me around. I talked to her..." He smiled softly to himself. "It was a bit exciting at times. Kristel van Daalen is an extremely beautiful woman, you know. In her own environment she has a sphere of influence." Dreamily he stared into the distance as if fascinated by his own thoughts.

Vledder looked searchingly at his old mentor, a slightly disturbed look on his face.

"And?" he asked.

Absentmindedly DeKok looked up.

"Oh, nothing. I mean, well, eh, I didn't get any further. That's to say I don't know any more than we knew this morning."

It was Vledder's turn to grin.

"Nanette Bogaard has disappeared, and beautiful Kristel expects the worst. That's the way it is, isn't it?"

"Yes. Yes, my boy, that's the way it is."

At that moment the phone rang.

Vledder answered, listened intently, then passed the receiver to DeKok.

"It's for you."

DeKok pulled his chair closer to the desk.

"This is DeKok. Who's calling?"

"Never mind that," said the voice at the other end of the line, "I just want to help you in the right direction is all."

"What direction...with what?"

"You'll find out, Mr. DeKok. I advise you to take a look on Mirror's Canal."

"Mirror's Canal?"

"Yes, the quiet side of the water."

"And what will I find there?"

The line remained silent for a while. The caller was obviously deliberating.

"Are you interested in antiques?"

"Not especially."

"You might find them worth your attention. Goodnight, Mr. DeKok."

"Goodnight."

The caller hung up.

For several seconds DeKok remained motionless, the receiver still in his hand clamped to one ear. He was searching among the relics in the attic of his brain—a memory, a point of reference. He did not find anything that gave him a clue. He could not place the voice. The insistent buzzing of an occupied line broke his concentration. Softly he replaced the receiver.

"Who was it?" asked Vledder.

DeKok shrugged his shoulders.

"An unknown lover of antiques, I think. I was advised to take a look on the quiet side of Mirror's Canal."

"For what?"

"Antiques, I think. You'll find that both sides of Mirror's Canal are occupied by antiques stores, or stores that purport to sell antiques. They stand shoulder to shoulder." He stood up and shuffled over to grab his raincoat and decrepit little hat.

"I think we should take a look," he said.

"Now?" Vledder voiced his surprise.

"Why not?"

Vledder sighed.

"What if it's a joke?"

DeKok made a helpless gesture.

"Well then, at least somebody will be amused."

7

Vledder drove through the old inner city of Amsterdam. Nimbly, as bold as a taxi driver, he managed to squeeze the old VW through obstacles, streams of traffic, and the thousands upon thousands of bicycles.

On the passenger side DeKok was sprawled out in his seat. A happy smile played on his lips. He loved the unknown. It attracted him irresistibly. That was the main reason he reacted so spontaneously to the strange tip over the telephone. It was ridiculous if one stopped to think about it, almost like some boyish adventure. He wondered what he would find on Mirror's Canal. What did the mysterious caller want him to find? Would it connect to the disappearance of Nanette?

Past the town hall they turned along Emperor's Canal and waited patiently for the red light at the corner of Leiden Street. They parked shortly thereafter at the intersection of New Mirror Street and Mirror's Canal. Vledder dimmed the lights and turned the ignition off.

He looked at DeKok, who was pressing himself upright. Vledder's young face wore a glum look. He showed no desire to get out of the car. DeKok looked at him from the side.

"We're here, my boy," he said, engagingly. "Would you rather have gone on your date after all?"

Vledder leaned forward on the steering wheel.

"It isn't that. You know that. If necessary, I'm ready to go night and day with you, step by step and hour after hour, even if you want to go to the North Pole."

DeKok grinned expansively.

"Such loyalty!"

Abruptly Vledder turned toward him.

"Loyal, yes, loyal, that's me—however I'm also forthright. You see, I don't use dirty police tricks on my colleagues."

DeKok looked at him with amazement.

"Dirty police tricks?"

"Yes, dirty police tricks. If you had to know so urgently, I mean, if you really wanted to know how it is between me and my girl, you could have just asked me. It wasn't necessary to use any of your transparent inter-rogation tricks on me." He imitated DeKok's voice with devastating effectiveness: 'Does she wear underwear with the days embroidered on them?'" He snorted. "What do you care what sort of undergarments Celine wears?"

With difficulty DeKok managed to suppress a loud, boisterous laugh. It caused a slight pain in his chest.

"Oh, oh," he said finally, "so her name's Celine?"

"Yes," answered Vledder sharply, "and she isn't at all the sort of girl who you apparently envision."

DeKok turned in his seat and put a reassuring hand on Vledder's shoulder.

"Listen, my boy," he said convincingly in a fatherly tone of voice, "I really wasn't trying to satisfy any prurient curiosity, and I most certainly was not trying to practice any dirty police tricks on you. Please take my word. I'll explain everything later in more detail. As far as Celine is concerned, I'm sure she's a very dear girl. You most certainly seem to have fallen for her, and not just a little, either. I wouldn't mind meeting her."

Vledder looked at him suspiciously.

"You mean that?"

"Yes, you should introduce her as soon as possible," nodded DeKok. "How about next Sunday? I'll ask my wife to organize a little party."

Vledder's expression changed. It became happier and sunnier. He was obviously mollified.

"Yes, that sounds like a great idea," he said with sudden enthusiasm. "Yes, we'll do that. We'll come. You can count on that. Yes, we'll look forward to it."

Vledder's moods had a habit of changing rather quickly.

DeKok looked at him once more and his eyebrows started to vibrate, as if in preparation of their famous dance across his forehead.

"From where I sit," he said slowly, "this may well be the love of your life. Yes, love with a capital *L*." He nodded to himself.

"What do you mean?"

"You're already speaking in *pluralis majestatis*."

"In what?"

DeKok grinned.

"*Pluralis majestatis*," he lectured, "plural as in royal plural. You know, as in 'We, Edward, by the grace of God, King....' The press uses the same sort of plural form.

And old married couples, of course. It's a disease. 'We' this and 'we' that. After a few years of marriage it has been known to be incurable."

There was nobody in sight on Mirror's Canal. The roadways on both sides of the canal were pretty much deserted. A car would pass occasionally, its turn signal blinking as it rounded the corner. But other than that nothing stirred.

Vledder and DeKok divided the task. Alert, prepared for anything, each started at one end of the canal and approached the other. Nothing in particular attracted their attention. They met in the middle.

Vledder shrugged his shoulders.

"Nothing, absolutely nothing. I think somebody pulled a prank on us." He gestured at the dark houses around. "Perhaps they're watching us even now, laughing from behind a darkened window."

DeKok pushed his hat farther back on his head.

"I don't believe it's a joke," he said seriously. "We've only just skimmed the surface, so to speak. We were told to pay attention to antiques. We haven't done that yet."

"What do you want?" asked Vledder. "Do you really want to look in the storefronts of all these shops?"

"There seems no other way," nodded DeKok.

Vledder started to chuckle to himself.

"What are we looking for? Oil lamps, nightstands with wormholes, bed warmers, silver candlesticks, rusty weather vanes, chamber pots? What's your preference?"

DeKok looked at his pupil with a slightly disapproving look.

"Just think of this," he said patiently, "as a real tip and not a wild-goose chase. The tipster wants us to discover something. He wants us to see it."

"Understandable, but how do we figure out what?" Vledder grimaced.

"Simple. It's something we would not recognize at first glance but from which the tipster expects us to draw conclusions. You understand? It must be a recognizable hint no matter what direction it leads. We're looking for the clue, not necessarily the object. Otherwise the phone call would make no sense at all."

"Clear as mud, but it covers the ground," nodded Vledder. Sometimes he could mix metaphors with the best of them.

"All right then, you start from the side of Prince's Canal and I'll start from the other side. Look carefully. Look at everything you see and try to visualize if any of the items could contain a hint we can use. If something, no matter how strange, draws your attention, you call me."

"Okay, boss."

They separated and began to search, each on his own end of the short canal. Slowly they ambled from one store to the next. A wild kaleidoscope of old objects passed by them, displayed helter-skelter in dusty little shops, small storefronts, and even some basement windows. Again they met approximately in the middle.

"And?"

Sadly Vledder shook his head.

"I saw nothing in particular. And you?"

DeKok rubbed his hands over his face.

"No," he admitted soberly, "me neither. There were endless scales, statues, unmatched chairs, flowerpots, lanterns, frames, more statues. The same junk everywhere."

Vledder laughed.

"Come," he said cajolingly, "let's go home."

He took the grey sleuth by the arm and tried to pull him toward the car.

"Tomorrow is another day. It's been enough for today." He looked at his watch. "It's almost midnight."

DeKok could not be moved. He stood his ground, stubborn. He scratched underneath his hat.

"There's got to be something," he exclaimed, irritated. "There must be. That call was not for nothing. It absolutely had a purpose. I'm old enough to detect the difference between a serious call and a joke. It wasn't a joke." He pressed his lips together. "You know what?" he continued vehemently. "We need to keep looking. I'll look in the stores you have looked at and you take my half. Understand? There is no other way. We must have missed something."

"Okay, boss," answered Vledder, bored.

DeKok looked at him.

"One more '*Okay, boss*,'" he said sharply and suddenly full of menace, "and I'll pull a gun on you."

Vledder was shocked by the sudden change of tone.

"Oh, eh, okay…"

DeKok grinned at the reaction. He never carried a weapon.

"All right, my boy," he said with much more warmth,

"let's try it one more time. If we still find nothing, then we'll call it a night."

Again they shuffled from window to window, one antique display to another. Carefully they looked at the items. What could be significant enough to move someone to call the police? And who was the caller? Why so secretive?

DeKok thought it over. If only he could identify the tipster he would have a better idea as to what kind of clue was hidden among the junk. While his eyes scanned the windows, his brain worked on a different level. He was looking for an answer, not just a clue. But neither his eyes nor his brain could come up with a solution.

DeKok was suddenly startled into an awareness of his surroundings. Vledder was standing next to him, tapping him on the shoulder.

"Come on," he said seriously, "I think I found something."

"Where?"

"A couple of doors down."

Meekly DeKok followed his pupil. Vledder halted in front of an old canal house with a bluestone stoop. He pointed diagonally upward. There was no store window, not in the strict sense of the word. The house had obviously been a residence in the dim past and then was converted into a store. The window revealed a showroom. It was dimly lit, and the various objects were spread out in the shadowy space. DeKok had passed the window twice and had not noticed anything in particular. He looked along the pointing arm of Vledder.

"What are you pointing at?"

"The painting."

"Where?"

"On the wall, just above the antique pistols."

DeKok's glance traveled upward, and then suddenly he saw it. It was a large, somewhat dark painting contained in a heavily gilded broad frame decorated with scrollwork and arabesques. The canvas had been painted in a simple figurative style, allowing the contours to softly flow into the background of somber blue and intense purple. The painting was uncommonly fascinating, and DeKok could not understand how he could have missed it before.

It was a nude seated on a low old-fashioned sofa of red brocade with a backrest edged in a stylized curving black wood. The figure of the young woman had been painted with great tenderness. The nuances in the soft pink of the skin and the gloss of the long waving hair bore witness to the intense emotion and loving attention directed at the subject. Although the nude was depicted in realistic detail, there was no hint of either sexual provocation or stimulation.

On the contrary, the painting reflected an intense calm, a serene, almost exalted, modesty.

Utterly fascinated, DeKok was absorbed by the impressions of color and composition. His glance followed every line of the painting. A long, slender hand rested on one knee, the breasts swelled sweetly, the back arched slightly. The long gold hair served as a frame for the fine face, a face that struck him. He recognized it even more so because of the somber look in the eyes.

"Nanette," he whispered softly.

Vledder took a deep breath.

"Yes," he sighed, "Nanette Bogaard. That's what the tipster wanted us to see."

For a long time they both stood speechless. Their noses were almost flattened against the window. The exquisite painting kept them spellbound.

Vledder was first to break the silence.

"I wonder," he said softly, "who could have painted her against such a dark backdrop?"

DeKok did not answer at once. As if bewitched he stared into the distance. His coarse face was expressionless.

"That's it," he said after a while, "that's it exactly."

Vledder looked at him with surprise.

"What?" he asked.

"The 'Somber Nude.' I can't think of a better name for the painting."

DeKok sat down on the bluestone stoop of the antique shop. Broad and immovable, he was like a human Cerberus. He had a face uniquely like a good-natured boxer.

Vledder stood in front of him and looked down at his mentor. Unable to ripple his eyebrows, he frowned.

"You're surely not planning," he started in a suspicious tone, "to remain on guard here the rest of the night?"

DeKok rested his head in his hands, elbows on knees.

"I must have that painting," he said resignedly. "I must know who painted it."

Slowly he rose, took his notebook from his pocket, and wrote down the name and phone number of the proprietor.

"It's too bad," he sighed, "the good man doesn't live near, behind, or above this shop. Then we could reach him at once."

He motioned to Vledder.

"Come on," he said. "We're going to call him."

"Now? At this hour?"

"Why not? Antiques dealers, so I've been told, always stay up very, very late."

They drove back to the police station following the deserted streets and canals. As soon as they arrived, DeKok picked up the phone and called the antiques dealer. It took a long time before anyone picked up on the other end.

"Grevelen here," said a sleepy voice.

"Yes, this is Inspector DeKok, with a kay-oh-kay, from Warmoes Street station."

"Homicide?"

"Yes, but don't worry. I just want to let you know I'm interested in one of the paintings displayed in your shop on Mirror's Canal."

"You're interested in buying it?" The sleepy voice sounded confused.

"Yes, I would appreciate it if you didn't sell it right away. You see, I want to take a good look at it first. I'll be by your shop in the morning."

For a while there was utter silence on the line. After a moment the man inquired, "Say, Mr. DeKok, is there something the matter with that painting?"

"Why?"

"Well, you're the second person to call me about it."

"The second?"

"Yes, there was a very excited man who wanted to buy the painting unseen, regardless of price. I thought it rather strange and all. I didn't take the call very seriously."

"Who was the man? Do you know?"

"Yes I do. Just a moment. I wrote it down somewhere."

The statement was followed by a few seconds of silence that seemed like an eternity to DeKok. Then the dealer came back on the phone.

"Here it is," he said. "Yes, that's who called. A fellow by the name of Wielen."

8

The next morning DeKok arrived late, as had been his habit for many, many years. As he walked in, Vledder met him halfway across the large detective room.

"Frank Bogaard," he began excitedly, "is gone! Last night he fled from the hospital. The commissaris wants to see you at once."

DeKok gave him a friendly nod.

"Good morning," he called cheerfully, "slept well, did you?"

Vledder swallowed.

"Last night," he tried again, "Frank Bogaard fled..."

Unperturbed, DeKok passed him by.

"Coffee ready?"

"Yes, that is, eh, I think so."

"Excellent," warbled DeKok exuberantly. "Excellent, really excellent."

He went to his desk, took his mug from a drawer, ambled over to the coffeepot, and poured calmly. Like most old-guard police officers on the force, DeKok lived by the golden Amsterdam rule: the day starts with coffee or not at all. It was a habit that could simply not be broken. The failure to solve a murder case, in a manner of speaking, was not nearly as serious as breaking the tradition of the renowned old station.

DeKok stirred an exorbitant amount of sugar into his coffee and sat down at his desk. Apart from tradition, he regarded coffee as a sort of tonic, an elixir capable of delivering both strength and inspiration. He enjoyed it luxuriously. An impatient Vledder stood next to his desk. DeKok looked up at him and savored his restlessness along with his coffee.

"What's the matter, my boy?" he asked in mock surprise. "Haven't had your coffee yet?"

Vledder snorted.

"Coffee, coffee," he grumbled, "by all means, coffee first. The commissaris said you were to report to him immediately! Not after an extended coffee break." He made a jerky, irritated gesture. "Furthermore," he continued, "I'd have thought you would find the news of Bogaard's escape from the hospital rather important."

Comfortably, DeKok continued to sip his coffee.

"Listen to me," he said, placing his mug in front of him, "one does not escape from a hospital. A hospital is not a prison. At most one could conclude Frank Bogaard did not appreciate the medical facilities available to him."

"It's the same thing. In any case Frank jumped out of a window and disappeared down the street in his pajamas. The crew of a patrol car saw him this morning near the Leiden Woods. A man in nightclothes does draw some attention, after all."

"And?"

"They put him in the car and delivered him here—he's downstairs."

DeKok looked surprised.

"Here? But why didn't they take him straight back to the hospital?"

"He didn't want to go. He most emphatically did not want to return to the hospital unless he had spoken with you first."

"Me?"

"Yes, he's downstairs waiting for you."

With one last swig DeKok drained his mug and stood up.

"Come on," he said, "let's go and hear what Frank has to say."

Vledder looked at him in astonishment.

"But what about the commissaris?"

DeKok pointed at the large clock on the wall.

"The commissaris has no time for me right now."

"No time?"

DeKok shook his head.

"It's ten o'clock. The commissaris is having coffee."

Their fellow officers had taken Bogaard to one of the interrogation rooms. That is where they found him. Frank Bogaard presented a shivering, shaking picture of human misery as he leaned against the radiator in the corner. He looked ridiculous in a wrinkled suit (left over from a drowning) and an old uniform overcoat from a sergeant long-since retired. A friendly constable had taken pity on him, issuing whatever clothing the station offered. Bogaard had looked so cold in his pajamas, suffering symptoms of withdrawal. But it did not help much. He was still shivering.

DeKok and Vledder entered the room, but Bogaard was barely able to look up. DeKok took a chair and straddled it backwards, his arms resting on the chair back. He had a gut feeling the seriously ill young man was the key to the riddle created by Nanette. He just did not know yet how the key would fit. It was still all so mysterious, so…ethereal.

"Why didn't you stay in bed? It's rather dumb to start roaming the streets in pajamas, especially in the middle of the night." DeKok's tone of voice was friendly, confidential. "If you wanted to speak to me I would have gladly come to you."

Frank looked up. It was as if he were just now noticing the presence of the two detectives. He looked from Vledder to DeKok, a haunted look in his eyes.

"Where is Nanette?"

DeKok shrugged his shoulders.

"I don't know. Nanette has disappeared. I told you so yesterday."

The young man flicked a quick tongue along his dry lips.

"Yes," he said tonelessly, "you told me she had disappeared. Nanette has disappeared, you told me. She's…" He kept repeating the same phrase over and over with slight variations. It was monotonous, as if he were trapped in a single thought.

Suddenly he seemed to free himself from the spell of his own words. His face gained some liveliness and the dullness receded, but soon his expression turned into a look of fear. He gripped DeKok's arms.

"You must find her, Mr. DeKok," he said quickly

in a hoarse voice. "As soon as possible. You must find her...you must."

DeKok gave him a penetrating look.

"Why?" he asked sharply. "So that she can supply you with your next fix?"

Bogaard's mouth fell open. Then he started to grin idiotically.

"How'd you know Nanette is my—"

"Your supplier?" offered DeKok.

Bogaard released DeKok's arms, turned, waved his arms in the air, and sank down on a chair.

"But the-then you must understand," he stuttered. "Y-you must understand she is in grave danger. Every minute is important. You mustn't lose a moment. You must find her before... before it's too late."

DeKok rubbed his nose with the back of his pinky finger.

"Too late?"

Bogaard's face contorted in fury.

"Yes," he screamed, "too late! There are no more ruthless people than drug dealers. You must know that. They're scum, all of them—bloodsuckers, poisonous snakes, hyenas, vultures."

DeKok pulled on his lower lip.

"Who," he asked, "delivered the drugs to Nanette that she in turn delivered to you?"

Frank Bogaard shrugged his shoulders.

"I don't know," he answered morosely.

"She never discussed it with you?"

"No, never."

"And you never asked?"

"No!"

DeKok sighed.

"You must have heard her mention a name at some point."

Frank hesitated momentarily.

"No."

"Think hard."

"*No!*" he screamed.

DeKok pressed his lips together. He knew the young man was lying. He felt he knew more than he wanted to say. Slowly DeKok rose, gripped Bogaard by the lapels of his coat, and lifted him out of the chair.

"What did you pay Nanette for the stuff?"

"Nothing."

DeKok took a firmer grip and pulled the young man closer.

"What," he asked intensely, "did you pay her for the stuff?"

Bogaard swallowed.

"Nothing. Really, I've never paid her a single solitary nickel for it."

DeKok's eyebrows started their dangerous ripple.

"Why not?" The tone was incredulous.

"She didn't want any money."

"What did she want?"

"Nothing," he screamed, "she wanted nothing."

DeKok snorted contemptuously.

"Oh, yes. Nanette, sweet angel of mercy, distributes free dope among the poor, tired, and huddled masses." His voice dripped with sarcasm. "Was it mercy or was it something else? Love, for instance, pure love for Cousin Frank? Is that it?"

Bogaard turned his head and did not answer.

DeKok was getting angry.

"Is that it?" he pressed. "Love?" He pronounced it like a curse.

Frank's eyes were red rimmed. His eyeballs started to glaze. Hot tears dribbled on his cheeks, dripped on the back of DeKok's hand. They seemed to burn like drops of hot metal.

DeKok's grip became less tight. He looked in the pale, unhealthy face of young Bogaard. He looked at the tears, his soft, slightly weak facial features. Suddenly DeKok noticed how much he and his sister, Kristel, had in common. It made him less angry.

"Sit down," he said softly. "How about a cup of coffee?"

Bogaard pulled his coat straight and sank down in the chair.

"I'd rather have a cigarette."

DeKok presented an opened pack that he usually kept for moments like these.

"Sometimes I may appear a little less friendly," he apologized. "Not because I want to be, you understand, but because it's my job."

A trace of a smile fled over Frank Bogaard's tired face. He lifted his right arm, causing the long sleeve of the old uniform coat to fall back to near his elbow. He accepted a cigarette with shaking fingers.

DeKok provided a light.

"I want to know *why* Nanette disappeared," he continued calmly. "Perhaps just maybe I can then discover *where*
she disappeared to. You see," he explained further, "I have
a feeling the two are connected, very closely linked. Mr.
Bogaard, an extremely important question: was Nanette a
poisonous snake, a vulture, a hyena, or an angel?"

Frank did not react at once. He lowered his head. He
thought about it, was obviously looking for the right way
to compose his answer.

"Most people," he said finally, "can be all those things
at the same time. It is repulsive. An incomplete composition with strange, shrill dissonants and shades of good
and evil."

"And what about Nanette?"

Frank pulled deeply on his cigarette. He looked at
DeKok through a heavy cloud of bluish smoke. His eyes
narrowed slightly.

"Nanette," he said with an unpleasant grin, "is a
poisonous snake in the shape of an angel."

DeKok rubbed his hands over his broad face.

"A classical disguise," he said with a trace of sarcasm.
"Very old—been in use from the beginning of time." He
made a slow, lazy gesture. "The daughters of Eve have
apparently little originality."

"But the apple became morphine," grinned Bogaard
bitterly.

DeKok looked at him silently for a long time. The
bitter remark had touched him. After a while he stood
up and pushed his chair back.

"We'll have you taken back to the hospital, Mr.
Bogaard. But you must promise not to indulge in repeated

nightly excursions. The doctors don't like it. It's also not conducive to your health." He placed a concerned hand on Frank's slender, shaking shoulder. "You must remember you have very little leeway for experimentation left," he concluded.

Bogaard looked up at him.

"What do you mean by that?"

"Your health is more undermined than even you suspect, Mr. Bogaard. A second nightly escapade may very well be fatal."

"Fatal?"

DeKok nodded with a grave face.

"I would like to see you stay alive."

Nonchalantly Bogaard shrugged his shoulders.

"Why?" he asked.

"A young, promising author..." DeKok gestured vaguely.

Frank sighed deeply.

"You mock me."

DeKok shook his head.

"No, not me," he answered sharply. "I don't mock you. You mock yourself. You're playing with your life *and* Nanette's."

"Me?"

"Yes, you!" exclaimed DeKok with emphasis. "Every moment is valuable, as you said. That remains true. Frank Bogaard, who supplied Nanette with morphine?"

"I, eh, I don't know."

"You do know!"

The young man's eyes filled with tears.

"Really, Mr. DeKok," he begged, "please believe me.

I don't know. I really don't. In passing, almost by accident, I once heard her mention a name in connection with dope. Just once she spoke of a Brother Laurens. It just slipped out. When I asked her who that was, she laughed. She never told me."

DeKok raked his thick grey hair with his fingers.

"Who is Brother Laurens?"

9

Commissaris Buitendam wore a perplexed frown. DeKok nervously entered his large office.

It was a pose, almost a game, and they both knew it. Neither fooled the other; they had known each other too long. Their association started in the almost forgotten past. Over the years the polite phrases had been twisted and modulated until they resembled a comedy. Although a farce, both performed it with utter seriousness.

"You wanted to see me immediately?"

The commissaris smiled thinly.

"Yes, about an hour and a half ago," he answered.

DeKok hung his head in shame.

"Sir, it is unforgivable. But I didn't want to disturb you while you were having your coffee."

The commissaris coughed.

"That is very considerate of you, DeKok."

"At your service, sir."

Buitendam coughed again.

"But I go so far as to presume that the coffee could not have been the only reason?"

DeKok shook his grey head and took a chair.

"May I?"

"But of course, please sit down and tell me all about it."

"I was engaged in an investigation."

"Connected with the girl who disappeared?"

"Indeed."

The stately commissaris searched among the papers on his desk.

"That's what I wanted to discuss with you. I read the telex message, the APB. It must be here somewhere. What was the name again?"

"Nanette Bogaard."

"Oh, yes. Nanette Bogaard. Here it is." He waved a copy of the APB in the air. "What's the situation? Are you making progress?"

"It is rather a confusing story. I honestly have to confess that I don't understand it at all. The how and the why of her disappearance is still a complete mystery."

"Clues?"

Shyly embarrassed, DeKok scratched the back of his neck.

"Too many, far too many. That's the difficulty. The further I get, the more I have the feeling I'm being led astray, or at least I am getting further away from the solution. It may sound contradictory, but that's the case."

The commissaris nodded his understanding.

"What about a release to the press, the radio or even TV?"

DeKok waved away the suggestion.

"No, I'd rather not, at least not yet. You know how it goes. One such release breaks all floodgates. We'll be following up on a veritable avalanche of tips, most if not all false or misleading. One person saw her in the north,

another in the south, some saw her in Paris, or Lord
knows where. There is no end to it. Only if I've really
reached a dead end, if there's no progress to be made any
other way, then and only then should we consider that
approach."

Slowly Buitendam nodded agreement.

"Have you any idea where she could be?"

"Not the slightest."

"How much longer do you think you'll need to find
her? I mean, if the judge advocate asks me…"

DeKok shrugged.

"If she's still alive."

The commissaris gave him a searching look.

"What do you mean?"

"Exactly what I'm saying. If she's still alive. I cannot
rule out the possibility that Nanette Bogaard is no more.
I'm almost certain she has been murdered."

"Murdered?"

DeKok rubbed his face with both hands. It was a
profoundly weary gesture.

"Yes, murdered. It's really the only reasonable explanation for her sudden disappearance."

Thoughtfully the commissaris looked at his
subordinate.

"Murder," he said finally, "requires a motive."

DeKok nodded.

"A motive *and* a body. But as long as we haven't found
Nanette Bogaard, dead or alive, we can't be positive.
For the time being it seems best to continue to follow
all clues, expand the investigation. We'll find out soon
enough where it will lead us."

"All right, keep me informed."

"But of course."

Both stood up and walked toward the door.

"Was, eh, is Nanette a good-looking girl?"

DeKok made an awkward gesture.

"Yes, according to our modern ideal, she's beautiful. Rubens would not exactly have laid awake nights over her."

The telephone rang. Smiling, the commissaris turned, picked it up, and listened.

"It's for you."

DeKok accepted the receiver and recognized the voice of the antiques dealer, Grevelen. There was an excited voice in the background. He was talking, trying to calm someone.

"Hello?"

"Inspector DeKok?"

"Yes."

"Mr. DeKok, I request you come here immediately. At once! I'm in the shop on Mirror's Canal."

"Why at once? What's the matter?"

Grevelen swallowed hard.

"There's a man here who demands the painting."

"What?"

"Yes, he claims that the painting is his property. Somebody must have stolen it from his house a few days ago, complete with frame and all."

DeKok thought quickly.

"Don't let him go. Keep him there."

DeKok threw the receiver down and ran from the office. The commissaris looked after him, astonished.

DeKok waved goodbye.

In the corridor nearing the stairs he started to call for Vledder.

"Vledder, Vledder, Vledder!"

His deep bass voice echoed through the building.

The old antiques dealer was waiting on the stoop in front of his shop, wringing his hands. Small red spots of excitement colored his lean, hollow cheeks.

"I'm so glad you're here," he said, relieved. "The man is furious." He laughed nervously. "He wanted to take the painting with him. Just like that. He cursed like all the devils from hell when I told him he had to wait for you."

"Where is he?"

"Still inside. I kept him for you. One of my staff is guarding the door."

DeKok nodded approvingly.

"Excellent, very excellent. We'll see what he has to say for himself."

Followed by Vledder and the scared antiquarian, DeKok entered the shop. The old sleuth appeared big, broad, and imposing. Fleetingly Vledder thought about the proverbial bull in the china shop.

An older man was standing toward the back of the shop. Next to him was an alert young man in the traditional grey coat of a warehouse worker. DeKok took another look at the older man. A well-preserved fifty or so, he estimated. His face was tan, his hair grey at the temples. The man was elegantly dressed, perhaps a little too youthfully, in a light blue suit of a particular modern cut with an excess of trim. He wore a small white rose as a boutonniere.

"This is an outrage—ridiculous!"

DeKok halted in front of the man. He stood in a particularly insolent manner: legs apart, shoulders square, head slightly cocked. A faint smile appeared on his face, almost mockingly.

"My name is DeKok. That's DeKok with, eh, a kay-oh-kay. This is my colleague, Vledder. I think you have already had the pleasure of Mr. Grevelen's acquaintance?"

The man murmured something that could be taken as a greeting. Then he pointed toward the wall.

"My painting," he blurted out excitedly. "Stolen!"

DeKok ignored the remark. Somewhat surprised, he looked at the man.

"I do not believe," he said with sweet sarcasm, "I have had the pleasure of making your acquaintance."

The man sighed.

"Staaten. Stockbroker."

DeKok made him the recipient of his sunniest smile.

"My pleasure, Mr. Staaten. So you're the man who claims that the painting over there is your property?"

"Indeed, yes. It is my property, stolen from my house."

"Stolen?"

"Yes."

"And have you reported the theft?"

"No."

"Why not?"

"Simply because I had not yet discovered the theft. You see, the painting was in my house on Emperor's Canal. Due to certain circumstances, I have not been there for the last few days."

DeKok nodded understandingly.

"Burglary?"

"No, no burglary. Only the painting was gone. When I came home late last night, I immediately noticed the empty spot in my living room. I missed it at once. I am very attached to the painting."

DeKok looked up past the antique pistols and rested his gaze on the painting.

"It is exceptionally beautiful," he said. Then, after a short pause, he continued, "How did you know so quickly the painting was here in this shop?"

Staaten hesitated momentarily.

"Somebody called me," he said finally.

"Who?"

"That, eh, that I don't know."

DeKok looked at him with sharpened interest.

"Strange, don't you think?"

The man shrugged his shoulders.

"I didn't really give it much thought. No, it didn't sound so strange. Shortly after I discovered the disappearance of the painting, a man phoned. He wanted to know if I had sold my *Nanette*."

"Your 'Nanette'?"

"The girl who modeled for the painting; her name is Nanette."

DeKok rubbed his flat hand over his face. He felt instinctively he should not keep asking questions much longer. The environment, the place, it was not conducive to a proper interrogation. He thought it especially ill-advised to elicit any confession from the broker in the presence of the dealer and his assistant.

"You understand, Mr. Staaten," he continued with a winning smile, "we cannot hand the painting over to you just like that. That's simply impossible. First, at the very least, we'll have to investigate this rather mysterious theft."

The detective turned to the antiques dealer.

"I assume, sir, you bought the painting in the normal legal manner, with the purchase registered in your books?"

Grevelen looked strangely at DeKok and then nodded.

"Oh, of course. Certainly," he said with emphasis. "My records contain the name of the seller, including the number of the passport he used as identification. I bought the painting myself."

"May I see the register for a moment, please?"

"But of course, I'll fetch it at once."

The old man walked toward the back of the store to his office and returned within seconds with a large book. He handed it to DeKok with a meaningful glance in his eyes.

"Please look on page seventeen," he said.

DeKok opened the book and turned pages. It was an exceptionally neat record. He had seen few like it. The purchases and sales were all noted, dated, and recorded in a minuscule but legible handwriting. The dealer seemed to be very detail oriented.

DeKok ran his finger along the entries on page seventeen. Almost at the bottom of the page he found it: *Painting, measuring 40 x 32 inches in gilded frame with scrollwork and arabesques, female figure, nude, on red brocade sofa, purchased from—*

Surprised, DeKok looked up.

"Who," he asked the sharp-dressed gentleman, "is Ronald Staaten?"

The broker's mouth fell open.

"Ronald Staaten?" he asked.

DeKok nodded.

With the back of his hand the broker wiped along his dry lips, looking suspiciously at DeKok. Finally he said, "Ronald is my son."

10

DeKok leaned both elbows on his desk. He looked at the stockbroker, his head resting on folded hands. He noticed a worried look on the tanned face.

"Please don't consider this a formal arrest, Mr. Staaten. On the contrary, I have merely asked you to the station in order to help the department with its inquiries. I want to know a little more about you and the painting. Also, you have to admit, the strange behavior of your son in regard to you and the painting requires a certain amount of explanation."

Staaten nodded slowly.

"I understand. However I don't think that I'm the one to give you much clarification."

DeKok gave him a winning smile.

"At least we can try. Together we'll see how far we can get. That is, if you're prepared to cooperate."

"Cooperate? To what end?"

"Well we can reasonably assume your son, Ronald, is responsible for the theft of the painting from your house on Emperor's Canal. The proof for this, you'll agree, is virtually incontrovertible. There are no signs of breaking and entering. The antiques dealer recorded the details of the sale. It is all rather straightforward. We could also assume you are not prepared to file a formal complaint against your son for the theft. You're not prepared to request formal prosecution, are you?"

Staaten shook his head vehemently.

"I should say not! That would be out of the question. Ronald is my only child. After the death of my dear wife, he's all I have left."

DeKok nodded his understanding.

"Exactly. As far as that is concerned, there is nothing for you to worry about, at least from me. If you don't file a complaint, we can't touch your son. Officially no crime has then been committed. Nevertheless I'm very interested in the motive. I assume that you, Ronald's father, are as intrigued as I am. Why would your son steal the painting and then sell it to an antiques dealer? Was he experiencing financial difficulty?"

The broker shrugged his shoulders.

"Ronald enjoys a generous allowance. And if he does need something extra, he has only to ask. I've never refused him anything."

"An enviable position for a son," smiled DeKok.

Staaten attempted a weary smile.

"I can afford it."

The grey sleuth pushed his chair back a little and stretched his legs. He would have loved to place them on the desk, as he sometimes did. But in the presence of a third person he resisted the urge.

"You like paintings?" he asked.

"Yes, I'm a collector and a connoisseur," nodded Staaten. "I own," he continued, "a considerable collection."

"Most are at Emperor's Canal?"

"Yes, it is my primary residence."

DeKok pushed his chair forward again. He leaned toward the broker. His sharp gaze was alert to every reaction.

"Why do you think Ronald would take that particular painting?"

Staaten stretched his neck and placed two fingers inside his collar, as if trying to get some extra air.

"That, eh, that I don't know."

DeKok stared at him searchingly.

"Really, Mr. Staaten," he said gently, "you really don't know why Ronald selected just *Nanette* of all your paintings?"

Staaten placed a hand in front of his eyes and rubbed their corners with a thumb and index finger.

"You're forcing me to say something I'd rather not."

DeKok shook his head.

"I am not forcing you to do anything. You're just afraid to face the truth. That's all. Your son picked the exact painting you valued most, am I right?"

The stockbroker sighed.

"You're absolutely right," he said finally, almost toneless and expressionless. "Ronald wanted to hurt me, punish me."

He paused, lost in thought.

"He's not a bad boy, Mr. DeKok, not at all. He's rather sentimental, sensitive like his mother. He was very much attached to her. They had such a strong bond, you understand. He was always more her son than mine. I didn't mind so much, although I would have liked to see him a bit more independent, more manly." Again he paused, then continued, "After my wife's death I feared Ronald would grow further and further away from me. Fortunately that did not happen. On the contrary, over the years we grew very close. We had a bond, too, based on mutual friendship and respect. We had almost an ideal father-son relationship. I could not have asked for more."

He sighed again, a weary sigh.

"But recently there have been some difficulties."

"Recently?"

"Yes."

"Why?"

Staaten did not answer.

DeKok rose slowly and came from behind his desk. He felt a certain pity for this man in his designer blue suit, a playful rose in the buttonhole.

"Why," he pressed, "were there difficulties between you and your son?"

Staaten bent his head.

"I, eh, I was planning to marry again," he whispered.

"Remarry?"

"Yes."

"And Ronald was against it? He disapproved?"

The man responded violently. With an abrupt movement he turned and looked DeKok full in the face. His cheeks turned red and his eyes spat fire.

"It's not up to Ronald to approve or disapprove," he said sharply. "I'm a free man! He's neither my guardian nor my conscience. I'm my own boss and fully competent to evaluate the consequences of my own actions. I'm not exactly senile!"

His tone changed.

"Listen, Mr. DeKok," he continued, calmer, "I have very dear and fond memories of my wife, but she's dead. The dead cannot consume the lives of the living. I'm fifty-five years old, healthy and virile. At least I am virile enough to be able to count on a number of happy years with Nanette."

DeKok arched his eyebrows in his own inimitable manner.

"Nanette...Nanette Bogaard?"

"Yes."

"The girl who modeled for the nude?"

"Indeed." Staaten moved restlessly in his chair.

"Do you know her?"

DeKok wiped his hand over his mouth.

"That's difficult to say," he said hesitantly. "I've never met her in person."

"I don't understand," said the broker, looking intently at the detective.

DeKok did not answer at once. He paced up and down the detective room for a while and thought about his answer. It was difficult to come up with the correct phrasing.

DeKok halted in front of the window. He assessed the man from a distance, a cool evaluation. In his own way Staaten was a handsome man, he thought. Certainly the type who would be attractive to a young girl. Nanette and the charming, debonair stockbroker probably met in Ye Three Roses while he was replenishing his boutonniere. It was on his way—the stock exchange is near the shop. One thing could have led to another... DeKok raked his fingers through his grey hair. Was this man responsible for Nanette's disappearance? Or perhaps the son?

DeKok came closer.

"How old is your son?" he asked.

Bristling, Staaten rose from his chair. His eyes narrowed and his lips were pressed together until they formed a thin line across the bottom part of his angry face.

"Ronald," he said, almost venomously, "is twenty-five years old. I know exactly where this is going. You're thinking as far as age is concerned, Nanette could have been my daughter."

Reproachfully DeKok shook his head.

"Please sit down, Mr. Staaten," he said calmly, soothingly. "Why are you so excited? I don't condemn you at all. On the contrary, I congratulate you and wish you all possible happiness. That's why I hope we will be able to find Nanette for you, as soon as possible."

The broker's eyes blinked. His face assumed an expression of genuine amazement.

"Find Nanette, you said?"

"Indeed, yes. Nanette Bogaard, you should know, seems to have disappeared."

"Disappeared?"

"Yes."

"How long has she been gone?"

"Since Thursday. She left the flower shop around three in the afternoon and nobody has seen her since."

A silence followed this statement.

It was obviously difficult for the broker to absorb the statement. All color drained from his face. Suddenly he looked years older—just a tired, worried businessman. After a long while he looked up.

"She left no message?"

DeKok sighed.

"You don't seem to grasp the situation, Mr. Staaten. Nanette is gone, and I don't think she went voluntarily. I'm afraid that something has happened to her, you understand? Something serious."

Staaten smiled sadly to himself.

"No," he said with a weary sigh, "nothing has happened to Nanette. Nothing serious, I mean. She's just fled. She has escaped from the consequences of promising to marry me." He shook his head as if to clear his thoughts. "I should never have asked her. I should never have forced the commitment." He sighed again. "She didn't want to hurt my feelings, that's all, didn't want to refuse me. That's why she agreed. It isn't her fault. I should have been wiser."

DeKok's eyebrows formed an interesting shape. It was too bad Staaten was not in the mood to appreciate it.

"You think that she's disappeared in order to escape a promise of marriage?"

"Yes, absolutely. There is no other explanation. Nanette has simply realized the age difference. She's just scared." He smiled a bitter smile full of irony. "After all, I'm not exactly a young Adonis," he concluded.

All this time young Vledder had leaned against a far wall almost unnoticed. He had listened carefully to the conversation between DeKok and the stockbroker. Not a single word, not even an inflection had escaped him. Slowly a theory had formed in the back of his mind, and slowly it took on more substance. He looked at his old mentor and waited for an opening.

DeKok saw his eager look and nodded permission. He walked over to the window and gave his pupil room to continue the interrogation of Staaten.

Vledder came closer.

"How did you envision the marriage between you and Nanette, Mr. Staaten? Were you planning a prenuptial or postnuptial agreement? After all, you're a wealthy man. Were you planning to marry Nanette under the community property laws, or were there going to be certain safeguards?"

Confused, he looked at Vledder.

"Well, eh, to tell you the truth, I never really thought about it."

"Perhaps not you, but others?"

Staaten's face became expressionless.

"You mean…"

"Ronald is your only son, your sole heir."

Staaten reacted strongly.

"What are you trying to imply?" His voice was sharp and challenging.

Vledder smiled faintly.

"Based on your reaction," he said calmly, "you know exactly what I'm trying to suggest, Mr. Staaten. With you marrying Nanette, Ronald would be an injured party, in a matter of speaking. At the very least he would lose a great part of his inheritance. If we're looking for a motive connected with Nanette's disappearance, then your son—"

Wildly gesticulating, Staaten jumped to his feet. In a blind, uncontrollable rage he took his tormentor by the throat and pressed down on Dick Vledder's windpipe. It blindsided Vledder, and for a moment he was too shocked to move. But all at once he sprang into action. The elder Staaten was no match for the young, athletic Vledder. With a quick movement he took hold of the stockbroker and pushed him away.

DeKok came closer, visibly upset. He pushed Vledder aside, took the shaking broker by the arm, and led him to another room. There he placed him on a chair and gave him a glass of water.

"You must control yourself, Mr. Staaten," he said sternly and reprovingly. "My colleague only made a suggestion, a *reasonable* suggestion. It was not an accusation."

He pressed the glass of water on him.

"Here, have another sip. When you have calmed down, you're going home. Once there, ask your son to contact us. I must put a few official questions to him."

Staaten looked at the old inspector.

"Are you going to arrest him?"

DeKok rubbed his hand over his chin.

"Why should I? Did he kill Nanette?"

11

Vledder stood in front of the mirror and looked at the red streaks on his neck. DeKok stood behind him, looking over his shoulder.

"How is it, my boy?" he asked with concern. "Does it hurt?"

Vledder shook his head.

"No, no, it doesn't hurt," he answered, irritated. "Not much, anyway. It just looks terrible, worse than it is. Tonight I'll have to explain it all to Celine. There's no way she won't notice."

"And," said DeKok, slightly mocking, "will she be overly concerned?"

Vledder turned abruptly. "Do you find that strange? Celine being concerned for me? She isn't at all happy about my assignment with you here at homicide. She's heard from some of our colleagues that you have a habit of getting involved with all sorts of strange cases. She's afraid, really."

DeKok snorted.

"Some of our colleagues are just like old women. They talk too much. But if you'd rather have another partner, that can be arranged."

Vledder's face changed under the influence of conflicting emotions.

"No, DeKok," he said shocked. "I don't mean it that way. I don't want another partner. On the contrary, I couldn't have found a better partner. There's nobody I'd rather work with."

"You flatter me," grinned DeKok. "Indeed you flatter me."

Vledder rubbed his neck again.

"Staaten has a considerable amount of strength in those skinny fingers. Dammit, it was like a steel trap. If we ever find out that Nanette was strangled, we'll know who the perpetrator was."

"And I rather thought that you favored his son as a suspect."

"True, I do. So far he's the only one with a clear motive. Ronald was interested in making Nanette disappear. You know," he said suddenly, "Staaten realized immediately how strong a motive Ronald has. It literally ambushed him. That's why he became so angry."

DeKok nodded.

"He reacted from a sense of guilt."

"Guilt?"

"Yes, guilt. If you ask me, Staaten felt guilty about his amorous relationship with Nanette. And he felt guilty about the marriage proposal. For a man concerned with public opinion it was tantamount to sin...certainly against the customs and mores of society. His attitude during the interrogation points to it as well. He was constantly in a sort of aggressive, adversarial position, as if we were accusing him and passing a moral judgment. He defended his relations with Nanette, although there was no reason to do so at all. Neither you nor I even hinted at it." DeKok paused, as if gathering his thoughts, then continued his impromptu summation. "But his sharpest reaction came later. His most aggressive behavior didn't surface until you pointed out that his relationship with Nanette might appear detrimental to the welfare of his son. The idea that his son might conceive of murder rather than accept Nanette as his stepmother opened a floodgate. Intellectually he had no defense, no reasonable argument against it. That's why he attacked you."

DeKok remain silent. For a while he stared at nothing in particular.

"It is always, eh, difficult," he continued slowly, "perhaps even dangerous to try and analyze someone's reactions and to use that analysis to come to a conclusion. This is especially true when one is not familiar with the background. It becomes speculative. But in my personal view, Staaten's attack on you was a sort of confession, an admission of guilt. In his heart, in his deepest thoughts, he has already considered your suggestion and believes it to be possible." He raised a finger into the air. "You must keep in mind that Staaten is an intelligent man. Don't forget he's a stockbroker, someone very capable of weighing a number of different factors and drawing a sound conclusion—the right conclusion, more often than not, or he would not have been able to amass such a fortune."

Looking at his finger as if surprised to find it there, he used it to rub the bridge of his nose.

"He must have considered all the pros and cons of his intended marriage to Nanette, and his son must have been an important part of his deliberations. When you offered the possibility that Ronald might have a valid motive for killing Nanette, I half expected him to counter with a superior attitude. The worst I anticipated was an arrogant smile, as if you'd uttered something off the wall. But he didn't do that, you understand. He did not reject your suggestion. He reacted as he did—quickly, furiously, guilt ridden."

Vledder looked at his mentor with wide eyes.

"Yes, yes, I understand," he answered, shaken. "Staaten did not ridicule the suggestion, because he's very well aware that his son is capable of murder."

DeKok nodded slowly.

"Indeed, that's the way I see it. And we'll have to keep that in mind as we progress."

Suddenly Vledder laughed loudly.

"I can't help it," he grinned, "but I think it's a strange case, all in all."

"Why?"

"Well, we run from one clue to another, we see suspects behind every corner, and hold long, philosophical conversations about all sorts of possibilities, but if you think about it, nothing has really happened yet."

Surprised, DeKok looked at him.

"A girl has disappeared, remember?"

"Well yes, but was there a crime?"

"Listen to me, son," DeKok sounded resigned. "Theoretically there's always a chance we'll find Nanette unharmed. But the longer this investigation goes on, the longer she's gone, the less I believe it. More than a day has passed, and we have been unable to get any proof of a *living* Nanette. On the contrary, we've found quite a few indications that a number of people might be interested in a *dead* Nanette." DeKok sighed deeply. "It sounds sinister, but that's the way it is."

Vledder countered, "You said a *number* of people, plural. Apart from Ronald Staaten, I don't see anybody else having a motive. There are more, you think?"

"Most certainly. For instance, have you forgotten Brother Laurens? Who's that then?"

"You refer, I presume, to the name mentioned by Frank Bogaard. According to him, he heard the name in connection with drugs."

"Exactly. But because of this painting business, he's been moved to the back burner. Regardless, I'm still very much interested in Brother Laurens as a possible suspect."

"A possible suspect?" scoffed Vledder. "You don't even know who he is."

"That's not necessary. I mean, even without knowing Brother Laurens we can come to a number of interesting, almost obvious conclusions."

"Such as?"

DeKok sat on the corner of his desk. His relatively short legs swung back and forth. Amused, he looked at young Vledder, a gentle smile on his craggy face.

"Think, my boy," he said. "Think hard!"

"What is there to think about?" asked Vledder, irritated. "We don't even know if Laurens is a first name or surname."

Approvingly, DeKok nodded.

"Very good," he said encouragingly, "very good. Both are possible, and we're only guessing at the spelling.

It could be Lawrence, Lorentz, or Laurens, the more common Dutch spelling. What about the term *Brother*? Where do we normally use that appellation in front of the name?"

Vledder grimaced.

"We'd use it in the religious sense, for a monk. Otherwise, maybe for a member of a fraternity or union. Perhaps even a family relationship."

DeKok shook his head.

"I was thinking of a different connection altogether."

"Not religious? No other kind of brotherhood?"

"No."

Suddenly Vledder's face cleared.

"I have it—in medicine! Of course, a nurse is often referred to as 'sister,' especially with all the English influence in the language. Now there are more and more male nurses, so people might refer to one of them as 'brother.'"

"Excellent. And what is the occupational residence of a male nurse?"

"That's easy, usually a hospital, sanitarium, maybe a rest home."

DeKok pushed his lower lip forward.

"Now think of drugs."

"Dammit, yes!" exclaimed Vledder enthusiastically. "You're right—hospital, drugs, morphine. Brother Laurens, that's it! A male nurse must be Nanette's supplier. It's the only answer, the missing link. Brother Laurens steals the morphine from whatever hospital he works in, passes it on to Nanette, who supplies Frank to help him with his writer's block."

DeKok laughed at Vledder's enthusiastic tone and excitement. He raised a cautioning finger in the air.

"As usual," he grinned, "you're much too eager. You're overlooking a number of important questions."

"Questions?"

"Just think a moment. Why would Brother Laurens deliver drugs to Nanette? Why would he run the risk?"

Vledder stared at his mentor with a questioning look on his face.

"I don't know, why?" he asked finally.

"Well remember, Nanette wasn't—*isn't*, if we still want to assume she's alive—interested in money. She couldn't have cared less about it, or so we've been told. Frank Bogaard told us she didn't want any money from him, and I believe him." DeKok lowered his finger. "So how could Nanette afford that?" he continued. "I mean, financially? As far as we know she didn't have any money of her own. Her sole capital was her share in the flower shop. You'll recall Kristel is the financial manager. She simply didn't have the funds. Yet she supplied Frank regularly."

"Okay then," Vledder nodded in agreement, "so you're telling me Brother Laurens's reward was something other than money? Money wasn't his motive for accommodating Nanette?"

"Exactly. So I repeat, why did he supply Nanette? Was he in love with her? Or was Nanette blackmailing him?"

"Blackmail?"

DeKok nodded. His face was serious.

"Yes. If we consider Frank Bogaard's physical condition, or rather his physical deterioration, Nanette has been supplying him for some time. He's been using for at least a year, maybe more. Something has compelled our Brother Laurens to continue to deliver considerable quantities of morphine, and remember that even after just a short period of time this becomes more and more dangerous. The chance of getting caught increases with every theft. Apparently Nanette had a very strong hold over Brother Laurens. I only know one explanation for such a strong hold over a person: blackmail!"

DeKok made a careful gesture, and then continued. "However that doesn't explain everything, not by a long shot. First we have to track down Brother Laurens and then determine what Nanette used as blackmail, if that's what it is. Of one thing I'm certain: Brother Laurens too had an excellent motive to kill Nanette."

Grinning, Vledder shook his head.

"All in all I keep thinking that this is a very strange case." He chuckled and offered, "We don't even have a corpse, but the list of suspects grows exponentially."

DeKok did not answer. He was not at all happy with the way Nanette's case was unfolding. It was a bit too unorthodox, too peculiar. He was wondering how to proceed. Young Vledder was right, it was all very strange.

A beautiful, young girl had disappeared...vanished just like that on a rainy day in July. *Why* had she disappeared? *Who* was this girl underneath it all? Carefree with a love for art and literature, if one believed Cousin Kristel. Barry Wielen, her would-be lover and a journalist, described her most enthusiastically as a "wild daisy from Ye Three Roses." A different description was added by Cousin Frank Bogaard, who bitterly described her as a poisonous snake in the shape of an angel.

DeKok scratched the back of his neck. Who to believe? Which version was true? It was a puzzle with pieces that didn't fit. Amid the contradictions an unknown, talented painter had seen a completely different side to Nanette. He presented a portrait not of a carefree girl or a poisonous snake. She appeared as a darling young woman with a soft, sad look in her eyes.

At once DeKok jumped off the desk.

"Come on," he said to Vledder, "we're going to do the rounds with the painting."

"Where to?"

Before DeKok could answer, the phone rang.

Vledder picked it up and listened.

He replaced the receiver after a few minutes. His face went ghostly pale.

DeKok looked at him searchingly.

"What's the matter?" he asked.

Vledder swallowed with difficulty.

"At the garbage dump near Canal F, they found the pieces of a young woman."

12

Just outside Amsterdam, past the Western Harbor, is a series of canals. The canals form a grid. The municipal garbage dump surrounds the canals, which were expressly dug for the purpose. Most of Amsterdam's garbage is amassed via collection trucks and barges, and all of it eventually finds its way to Canals A, B, C, and so on. These particular waterways are the only unnamed waterways in Holland. Each is designated with just a letter. In these impersonal canals the garbage is dumped, sorted, processed, and eventually converted into various kinds of fertilizer or relegated to landfills.

It had started to rain again. The wipers of the old VW, going at top speed, barely succeeded in keeping up. The view through the windshield was vague and distorted.

Vledder drove around the harbor until he found the entrance to the dump. From there a barely discernable road crossed the terrain. The road was only visible because it seemed to contain less garbage.Proceeding carefully across a swaying pontoon bridge, they reached the far side of Canal F. Steel plates indicated a path to a field, a wide, stinking field full of garbage.

Off to one side was a small town, a hole-in-the-wall really. "Rustic" was the name of the town. Considering its proximity to the garbage dump, it could hardly have been named less appropriately. Behind a misty veil, DeKok and Vledder could just discern Amsterdam between rain showers. The steel plates ended between two immense mountains of garbage. It was the end of the road. Vledder stopped the car. From a distance they saw a Caterpillar dozer and a group of men.

The two detectives got out of the car. Silently they approached the men. There were four broad and strong types from the Amsterdam Municipal Sanitation Department. Their weather-beaten, somber faces were shiny from rain. They moved out of the way. There was a dirty piece of canvas on the ground at their feet.

A slightly greying man, apparently the oldest of the group, looked up, turned to DeKok, and asked, "You're from homicide?"

"Warmoes Street," confirmed DeKok, nodding.

The man rubbed the rain from his face with the sleeve of his slicker.

"Just look," he said. His voice trembled.

He leaned over, took a corner of the canvas, and lifted it carefully. Slowly a head became visible, the roughly severed head of a girl.

DeKok felt the blood drain from his head. His stomach rebelled. He swallowed quickly and took a deep breath to suppress the inclination to vomit. He heard Vledder panting next to him. DeKok pulled the collar of his raincoat closer around his neck, trying to close the gap between the coat and his hat. It was an odd gesture. He just needed time to get over his revulsion. Any confrontation with death brought him to a confused halt. Despite his many years of experience and numerous encounters with violent death, he had never been able to get used to it. Usually he was able to hide his emotions behind an expressionless, cold facade. Bracing himself, DeKok moved to take a closer look at the head. He squatted down and took the fabric from the older man's hand, lifting the canvas slightly higher.

The face was waxen. The almost transparent skin was covered with dirt and crusts of coagulated blood. The long blonde hair was flattened by the rain and stuck around the neck, mercifully hiding some of the horror that was visible there. The head had been severed just above the torso. DeKok looked at the half-open eyes. Carefully he lifted the eyelids one by one. The irises were cornflower blue. He looked around. Within his grasp he found a few pieces of a broken clothes hanger. He picked up a piece and used it to lift the upper lip slightly and pressed down on the lower lip. Two rows of straight, pearl white teeth became visible. There were no fillings in the molars.

DeKok tossed aside the pieces of hanger. Mentally reviewing the description of the missing girl, he knew there was no doubt—none whatsoever—who this was. The severed head was that of Nanette Bogaard.

DeKok pressed his lips together. His fears had come true. Nanette had been horribly murdered. The murderer had even taken the time and the trouble to sever the head.

He looked at the man who was squatting down next to him.

"Is this all you found?"

The man shook his head.

"Over there," he said somberly, "is the rest."

Carefully, with a tender, almost devout gesture, he covered the girl's head with the scrap of canvas. Then he rose and walked away. DeKok, Vledder, and the others followed him. They walked slowly, silently, in single file. It was like a funerary procession in the rain. All that was out of place were the garbage and discarded household items. Their shoes sank in the mud, as if they were crossing a swamp. The damp stink of decay permeated everything. A couple of crows sheltered under a rusty furnace. As the men passed, the birds flew away, screeching loudly. A large yellowed doll missing a leg stared at the sky, displaying a soulless smile.

The older man halted next to a few pieces of cardboard sheltered by the bulldozer. He waited patiently for everyone to join him. They formed a circle. Then he removed the cardboard. The shock was slightly less this time.

Placed in one spot were the severed parts of the body: the arms; the long, slender legs; the petite torso. There was no clothing to speak of. The red nail polish on the toes stood out sharply against the pallid limbs. In contrast to the head, there seemed to be less dirt and blood on the remaining body parts. Apparently they had been lying in the rain a little longer and had been washed by it.

DeKok bent over to take a closer look at the disfigured remains. It seemed a professional with anatomical knowledge had been at work. There was no question of a hasty, panicky butchering. He had seen that too many times in the past. On the contrary, in order to remove the limbs from the torso, only the absolute minimum of cuts had been applied. Yes, concluded DeKok, this took more than a smattering of anatomical knowledge.

His glance drifted to the petite torso. As far as he could see there were no other outward indications of injury or mutilation.

DeKok remained in a squatting position for some time. Subconsciously his thoughts went to the large doll they had just passed, the doll with the frozen smile and the single leg. It had been thrown out. Children had played with it. They had walked with it. Had dressed it, undressed it, cared for it, until...

"My wife," he said suddenly, loudly, "still keeps the dolls from her childhood."

"What?" asked Vledder.

DeKok looked at him, confused, absentminded. He rubbed his eyes with a tired gesture.

"Nothing, my boy, nothing," he answered, evading the question.

He rose slowly and turned to the older man, apparently the foreman.

"Did you find all the remains?"

"Yes."

"What's your name?"

"Claus...Claus Boer."

DeKok turned to Vledder and signaled for him to take notes.

"What did you find first?"

The man from the sanitation department did not answer at once. He took the large pieces of cardboard and carefully covered the body parts.

"First I found a leg."

"And then?"

The man turned and gestured around.

"Look, mister, when the garbage is dumped from the trucks or lifted from the barges by the crane, we get heaps, big heaps, of garbage. The first task is to smooth it out. I use the bulldozer to distribute it equally, so to speak. Of course everything you can imagine is in the garbage. We find the craziest things. So we usually don't even notice all that spills out. It's all just garbage, you see. But this morning, suddenly I saw a leg sticking out of the dirt. At first I thought it was the leg of a mannequin, you know, a store dummy. That happens sometimes. But it looked so real, you know...too real. Well, I stopped the machine and took a closer look. It was for real, you know, a real leg, I mean."

"What did you do then?"

"I wanted to call the police right away. But we're sorta isolated here, you know. There's no phone nearby. It's a good twenty-minute walk from here to the main gate. So I decided to wait for somebody. There are no barges due today, but the trucks do come in all the time."

The man wiped the rain from his face, then continued.

"Anyway, I lifted the leg from the garbage and put it aside. A little later I found an arm. I really started to look then, you know. It wasn't too difficult. It took me less than fifteen minutes to find all the pieces."

"Did you find the head at the same time?"

"No, I found that later, you know. That was after, I mean after I had asked somebody to call you."

DeKok nodded.

"Did you find the pieces far apart?"

"No, I mean, not so far. They were all more or less, eh, within a thirty- to forty-five-foot area. Not farther, anyway. You know, I think it all came from the same truck."

"When, do you think?"

"Yesterday...yes, yesterday afternoon, I think. You see, we work alternately—alternate days. What is dumped today is equalized tomorrow, you know. Today I'm equalizing what was dumped yesterday, you see. I was working here, and here I found it. So it was dumped yesterday."

Slowly DeKok glanced around the enormous mountains of garbage.

"Mr. Boer," he said after a while, "do you have any idea where this particular garbage could have originated?"

"You mean, eh, the garbage with the body parts?"

"Yes."

"Well, that's a bit difficult to say, mister. It's probably from West. Yes, Amsterdam West. But where exactly, I don't know. Could be any one of lots of neighborhoods. Take your pick: Ditch Canal, Mill Lake, Ox Village, Halfway. Good luck figuring out exactly. If the load had come by barge, it might have been easier. The crane driver usually knows where the barges come from, but that's usually the old part of town, you know. West all comes by truck."

DeKok smiled faintly.

"That's quite an area. Half of Amsterdam lives in West."

The man made a helpless gesture.

"Yes, I understand," he said sympathetically. "Yes, I know, I mean, it's important for you to know where to start looking. You need that information. Believe me, I would be only too glad to help. The thing is, even if I knew exactly what truck had dumped that particular load, it wouldn't solve the problem, you know. I mean, the trucks we use today have a much larger load capacity than they once did. They cover large areas."

"Do you think it safe to assume the body parts, along with the garbage in which they were found, all came from the same truck?"

The sanitation man nodded emphatically.

"Oh, yes, that's correct."

"Thus I can rule out the possibility that the corpse, the pieces of the corpse, came to be here in any other way?"

"Absolutely."

"Excellent."

The closing of a car door made DeKok look around. A special unit of the municipal medical service was arriving. It was one of the units usually sent out for drowning incidents. There must have been a mix-up in the dispatch office. The coroner's van would have been more appropriate, although the crew seemed to know what was needed. The paramedics left the ambulance, approaching slowly. They carried a large galvanized kettle between them.

Vledder pointed at the body parts.

With impassive faces they gathered the head, arms, legs, and torso. As they placed them in the kettle, there was no sign of emotion. The sanitation workers looked ill.

"Please take everything directly to the pathology lab," said DeKok.

The older of the two paramedics nodded.

"You know the name of the victim already?" he asked.

"Nanette Bogaard," DeKok swallowed a lump in his throat.

The paramedic took out a notebook and wrote it down.

"Do you claim ownership in the name of justice?" he asked formally.

"Yes, my name is DeKok, with, eh, a kay-oh-kay. Homicide, Warmoes Street."

The paramedic closed his notebook and placed it in the breast pocket of his uniform coat. He and his colleague lifted the kettle between them and walked back to the ambulance. Their free arms swung back and forth to equalize the load.

After the ambulance had disappeared with its grim load, the older man took DeKok by the sleeve.

"Did I hear you mention the name of the girl?" he asked.

"Yes…"

The man hesitated.

"Was it…eh, was she a bad girl?"

DeKok looked at him searchingly.

The man was shamefaced and embarrassed.

"I, eh, I have a daughter. This girl's face…it reminded me a bit of my daughter, you know. Sometimes parents don't know what to do or think. We can't watch them night and day, you know." He shook his grey head and sighed. "No, not night and day. I just hope for the best a lot of the time."

DeKok placed a comforting hand on his shoulder.

"Just do that," he said encouragingly. "Hope for the best. Luckily only a few wind up in the dumps—literally, I mean."

He bent down. The large yellow doll with the missing leg was at his feet.

He picked it up. "May I have this?"

The sanitation man looked at him with surprise.

"But of course, go ahead."

"Thank you."

He turned and walked back to the police car. The doll swung from one hand.

Vledder followed.

13

Young Vledder floored the gas pedal of the old VW. He drove wildly, as one possessed. Leaning forward over the wheel with a determined look on his face, he forced the old car to the limits of its capabilities. The engine whined in protest.

DeKok looked at him from the passenger seat.

"What's the matter, my boy?" he yelled over the sound of the engine. "Why the rush?"

Vledder did not answer. Staring at the road he proceeded at an undiminished speed. The long road ran alongside the canal. At the end of the road he sideslipped onto the wet pavement of the main highway, barely missing a truck as it came from the opposite direction. Ignoring traffic, Vledder casually brought the skid under control as though it were a routine move.

DeKok shook his head and grinned.

"What are you trying to do?" he asked cynically. "Are you trying to overtake death, or are you fleeing it? It doesn't matter, you know. No matter what, death always wins in the end."

"Funny," spat Vledder. "Inspector DeKok makes jokes, real funny jokes about death."

DeKok pushed his lower lip forward, otherwise he

did not react. He had not meant to be funny, not at all. He'd meant it as a good-natured warning against speeding. He doubted Vledder had actually taken it as a joke. It was clear Vledder just needed to lash out at something, someone. He knew his pupil well enough to have some idea how he was feeling right now. The horrible discovery at the dump had touched him; it had disturbed his equilibrium, so to speak. DeKok had seen this before. The boy took things too much to heart. Besides being sensitive, he had not yet learned how to disassociate his emotions and feelings from the unpleasant aspects of the job.

Nearing the city they encountered the usual gridlock. They were able to proceed at barely a snail's pace. DeKok did not mind at all. He slid comfortably down in his seat and inspected the doll he had picked up at the dump. Vledder looked at him and grinned sarcastically.

"A young girl has been put to death in a most horrible way," he said. "So horrible that the pieces had to be gathered from all over the place. And what occupies the brain of the great sleuth?" He snorted derisively. "The great sleuth asks the garbage man, oh so politely, if he can please have an old, dirty broken doll."

He moved the car a few more feet and shook his head in desperation.

"Dammit, DeKok, there are more important things to be concerned about than an old doll with one leg."

"Such as?"

Vledder gave him an angry look.

"Such as solving the murder," he said tersely.

DeKok sighed a deep sigh.

"You see," he said resignedly, "that's exactly what occupies me at the moment."

Corporal Bykerk was acting as desk sergeant. As DeKok and Vledder entered the lobby of the old Warmoes Street police station, the corporal hefted his considerable bulk from the chair behind the desk.

"What about the report from the dump?" he asked. "Can I cancel the APB for the Bogaard girl?"

Slowly DeKok nodded.

"Yes, you may. We don't have to find her anymore. We found her in pieces...murdered." He grimaced in Vledder's direction. "All we need now is the murderer," he concluded.

Corporal Bykerk grinned.

"Is *that* all?" he asked.

"Ach," said DeKok, "it shouldn't take my partner too long."

Vledder looked angry. With a face like a thundercloud he turned and started to climb the stairs to the detective room. Bykerk called him back.

"There's somebody waiting for you in three," he called. "I think he can tell you a thing or two about the Bogaard girl. He's been waiting more than an hour already."

Vledder looked at him suspiciously.

"Who?"

Bykerk looked at his notes.

"One Ronald Staaten. He asked for Inspector DeKok, told me he came in connection with the disappearance of Nanette Bogaard. If your old mentor permits you to question him, he's in interrogation three. At least you could start the ball rolling."

DeKok nodded agreement.

"All right, it's a good idea. I have the feeling that our friend Vledder would just love to ask him a few penetrating questions. Isn't that so, my boy?"

Vledder growled something inaudible.

Bykerk laughed out loud.

Ronald Staaten seemed very sure of himself. As Vledder and DeKok entered the interrogation room he stood up, made a polite bow, and calmly reseated himself.

"My father," he spoke in an affected voice, "imparted to me the knowledge that the gentlemen of the police were vitally interested in my humble self." He made a small artistic gesture with his hand and showed two rows of even white teeth. "Well, as you perceive, here I am," he concluded.

DeKok nodded slowly.

"We can see that," he conceded. He pointed in the direction of Vledder.

"My colleague will ask you a few questions. You must understand that this is routine. But I strongly urge you not to take liberties with reality."

Staaten grinned.

"The truth and nothing but the truth?"

He seemed to be amused by his own wit. He crossed his arms in front of his chest and presented a picture of self-satisfaction.

DeKok rubbed his hand over his face.

"Truth," he said with emphasis, "is never a subject for jokes. It is seldom funny."

Ronald shrugged his shoulders nonchalantly and Vledder pulled a chair closer.

"You still live at home with your father?"

"Yes."

"Do you have any brothers or sisters?"

"No."

As Vledder started the interrogation, DeKok took the opportunity to study Ronald Staaten at length. Ronald, he thought, had little in common with his father. There was no similarity in either behavior or appearance. Ronald was a slender young man with blonde shoulder-length, wavy hair, green eyes, and soft, almost weak facial features. He was handsome in a slightly repugnant, effeminate way.

He portrayed an attitude of conscious challenge that was almost provocative. He was dressed in a deep-purple jacket with flowers and a light-colored pair of slacks. He answered Vledder's questions with an irritating smile.

"Do you get along with your father?"

"Do I have to answer that?"

"If you like."

"No."

"Why not?"

Ronald grinned; it was not a pleasant sight.

"What young man is able to coexist with his father? We tolerate each other. That is probably the most positive statement I can make regarding our relationship."

"That was different until recently?"

"What do you mean?"

"I understand from your father that you grew close after the death of your mother. He spoke of a good father-son relationship."

Ronald did not answer at once. He lowered his head somewhat. For the first time his arrogant manner seemed to leave him.

"What could I do?" he asked after a while. "He was the only person who was there for me. I could hardly ask for consolation from the neighbors, right? After all, he *is* my father."

Vledder hesitated a moment.

"That, eh, that sounds bitter."

"Yes!" Ronald Staaten's voice rose to a scream. "You're right! It sounds bitter. Have you any idea why my mother died? Well do you? No, of course not. You don't know anything. That geriatric Don Juan killed her! My mother died of shame, of humiliation."

"Humiliation?"

"Yes, she died humiliated by my father's affairs with hundreds of women—women of every age, color, race, type, you name it."

"And your mother knew that?"

Ronald nodded emphatically.

"My father even had the unmitigated gall, the inso-lence, to boast about his so-called conquests to others. He talked about it in my mother's presence. Just think about that, if you will."

He shook his head several times.

"My mother...my mother was a dear and gentle woman. She never said anything, never complained. She never openly objected to my father's behavior. She suffered in silence."

Vledder swallowed and pushed his chair back. Meanwhile he glanced quickly at DeKok, who was leaning against the wall out of Ronald's line of sight. An encouraging nod from his mentor convinced him that he should continue the interrogation in the same vein.

"Your mother confided in you?"

"Yes."

"So what she knew of your father's sexual adventures, you knew as well. You shared the knowledge?"

"Indeed. Mother had no secrets from me."

"Did you ever discuss divorce with her?"

"Mother didn't want a divorce."

"Why not?"

"For one thing, she had religious conviction. Mother was very devout. Also, she wanted to ensure my inheritance."

Vledder tried to raise his eyebrows.

"Ensure?" he asked.

"Yes, you understand, as long as the marriage between my parents was intact, I remained the sole heir. Mother wanted to keep it that way. Had she decided on divorce, Father would almost certainly have remarried. Who knows how many legal offspring would have been the result."

Vledder grinned broadly.

"Ah, yes, any of the brats would share in the spoils."

"That was an inelegant remark, to say the least," Ronald reacted sharply. "I would say insulting," he concluded.

A slight blush moved quickly over Vledder's face. The sharp tone of young Staaten did not, however, break the rhythm of the interrogation.

"But if I understand you correctly," he continued calmly, "it sounds as though you held your father responsible for your mother's death. Is that right?"

"Yes."

"You believe your father's bad behavior actually affected your mother's health?"

"Yes."

"Did you ever tell him that?"

Ronald sighed.

"No, I never told him. He never gave me the chance. It's as simple as that."

Momentarily confused, Vledder stared at him.

"I don't understand."

Ronald sighed again. It actually seemed heartfelt.

"After Mother died, I decided to tell him in no uncertain terms what I thought of him. It was about time someone told him the truth. As long as Mother was alive, I kept silent for her sake."

"And?"

Young Staaten rubbed a hand through his long hair. He shrugged his shoulders and made a defeated gesture.

"When the time came," he said softly and sadly, "I couldn't. To my chagrin, he showed real remorse. My mother's death really devastated him. It was disarming. I lost the incentive, you understand? He locked himself in his room and would not come out for days at a time. It was a sort of penance, or at least I thought."

Vledder looked at him searchingly.

"What exactly do you mean by 'thought'?"

The young man snorted contemptuously.

"Within a year of her death he was already pursuing a young girl."

"Nanette?"

"Yes," he answered absentmindedly. "Yes, Nanette Bogaard. One night they both came to see me, hand in hand. God, it was so revolting! My father announced in a trembling voice that they had come to an agreement and would soon marry."

Vledder stood up.

"And thus," he announced primly, "we arrive at the beginning of the drama. The drama of Nanette, or the struggle for the fatted calf."

14

Young Ronald reacted angrily. He pulled his lips together until they formed a thin, narrow line. His handsome young face showed hostility.

"What fatted calf?"

With his head slightly cocked, Vledder looked at him for some time.

"Come, come, Mr. Staaten," he said finally. His tone was friendly, patience evident in his words. "You know very well what I'm talking about...your father's rather extensive fortune."

"What does that have to do with it?"

"Everything! You couldn't have made it clearer; you're the sole heir. It was the express wish of your mother that this should remain so. Isn't that right? She was willing to suffer a life of shame and humiliation just to preserve the status quo. It is understandable that you, her son, would want to ensure your mother's wishes were honored. In other words, you'd make sure to remain the sole heir."

A tic developed on Staaten's left cheek.

"You, eh," he said carefully, "you're insinuating..."

"What?"

Staaten turned his head away from Vledder. He swallowed several times. His Adam's apple bobbed up and down.

"You're insinuating I have something to do with Nanette's disappearance?"

Vledder sniffed.

"To put it mildly," he said, "you have a convincing motive for murder."

With a shock the young man sat up straight.

"Murder?"

"Exactly. Murder. And you could save yourself and us a lot of trouble if you were to tell us right now, without unnecessary evasion, when and where you killed Nanette Bogaard."

Staaten's eyes grew large and afraid. He looked at Vledder in surprise. All he saw was an impassive face.

"Me?" he whispered.

Vledder nodded silently.

Staaten could not ignore the statement. There was no way out. Like an idiot, he started to grin nervously. All color drained from his too-pretty face. Scared, he looked around him. With a silent appeal in his eyes he looked from Vledder to DeKok and back again. His eyes mirrored an attitude of dog-like devotion.

"M-me?" he stuttered finally. "Nanette. That's, th-that's crazy! You cannot be serious! No, you don't mean it." He kept shaking his head. "NO!" he screamed suddenly. "Not me...not me!"

Vledder stood up. The denial did not affect him. On the contrary, Ronald Staaten appeared ready to confess. He judged the broker's son as having very little resistance left. He had only to persevere, or so he thought. Until now he had built the interrogation neatly, step by step, by the book. After establishing motive he had made an outright accusation. All he needed from Ronald Staaten were the details. Then the Nanette case would be solved. It would be his first great triumph.

From his standing position he looked down at the scared young man on the chair. The deep-purple, floral jacket was no longer a provocation. It was just ridiculous.

"At first," he began slowly, "I didn't understand why you took the painting of Nanette and sold it. I couldn't explain it. It seemed so senseless." He sighed heavily. "Now I understand. It is as clear as day. The painting had to go. You couldn't stand to see it anymore. The beautiful, perfect body on the canvas was a constant reminder to you of her death—the terrible, disgusting disfigurement you inflicted..."

Vledder had started to speak louder and faster as he progressed, building up to a climax in his recapitulation. His last words echoed against the bare plaster walls of the small room. In the silence that followed, Ronald Staaten looked stricken. He looked as if nothing had registered. Unaware of his surroundings, he stared in front of him. His mouth was half open.

Vledder became increasingly irritated. The blood rushed to his head, pulsating at his temples. Accusingly he stretched his hand out to young Staaten. It was a theatrical gesture.

"You," he yelled, "you killed her! Nanette was in your way. You saw your inheritance threatened. You didn't want your father to marry again. You suddenly realized how vital, how virile he still was." Vledder imitated Ronald's voice, mocking him. 'And who knows how

many legal offspring would have been the result of that.'
Those are your own words."

Staaten failed to react. He remained in a cloud of
apathy. The disconnection insulated him from the world
for the moment.

Vledder shook his head angrily. He felt himself losing
his grip. His words had not elicited the desired result. It
was so frustrating. He had been so close to triumph, and
now it was washing away like footsteps in wet sand.

Overcome, he took Staaten by the lapels of his jacket,
lifting him out of his chair. Vledder's anger seemed to
make him stronger. The silk-like fabric strained in his
grip.

"Why," he hissed, "did you sell the painting? Why?"
He shook Staaten the way a dog shakes a rat. "Dammit,
you bastard, open your mouth. Why did you sell the
painting? Answer me!"

The young man remained silent.

Vledder changed his tone. His eyes narrowed to slits.

"I'll answer for you," he said softly, threateningly. "It
was fear, pure fear. You were afraid of that nude portrait;
it was a constant reminder, an accusation on the wall of
your living room."

It seemed as if Ronald suddenly woke up. He looked
Vledder in the eyes. His gaze was clear and steady. Softly,
tonelessly, he said, "It was not fear. Not that at all."

The denial irritated Vledder even more. His eyes spat
fire. In a sudden explosion of near hysterical strength he
pressed Staaten against the wall of the interrogation room.
The chair was kicked out of the way and fell noisily in a
corner of the room.

"It was fear," he screamed at the top of his voice. "You're lying, it *was* fear. Tell me. Tell me!"

Vledder kept repeating himself. He was obviously beside himself. As he lost control, his voice broke.

DeKok saw the danger.

"Vledder!"

It sounded stern; there was condemnation in the voice.

"Let go of him and get out."

Vledder did not respond at once. It took a few seconds before DeKok's words penetrated. He closed his eyes tightly and shook his head as if to clear it. The red mist of rage that had taken control of him dissipated slowly. He let go of the young man. After a moment of stillness, he looked at his victim and murmured, "Sorry, really sorry." Then, head down, he left the room.

DeKok watched him go. He knew so well how his pupil felt at this moment...utterly miserable. He remembered his early days, when he was as young as Vledder and faced with an inevitable defeat. It was almost impossible to accept. But those days were gone. The years had made him more experienced. Above all, the years had made him wiser.

Sighing, he picked up the fallen chair.

"Please sit down," he said in his friendliest tone of voice. "Are you all right? Did he hurt you?"

Staaten smiled faintly.

"It wasn't all that bad."

DeKok made an apologetic gesture.

"My colleague is, eh, a bit short-tempered and overzealous at times. Please don't hold that against him.

Although his methods can be a bit unusual at times, he's after all fighting for the truth. He's fighting the good fight. I mean to say, his motives are pure." His faced creased into a friendly smile. He asked, "Wouldn't you agree?"

Young Staaten managed a sad grin.

"Pure?" he laughed mockingly. "What a choice of words. Your colleague wanted to force a confession out of me. Perhaps you consider that fighting the good fight, maybe you think that is pure. I regret to inform you, I do not share your opinion. His methods are contemptible."

He sank down in the chair, crossed his legs, and rubbed both hands through his hair. Apparently he had recovered from Vledder's attack. His face had regained some color. He gestured in DeKok's direction.

"How can I possibly confess to something I haven't done? That's too crazy, don't you agree? Nanette is dead, according to your colleague. She's been murdered. It's tragic, but I did not do it. If you want to hold me responsible for her death, then it is strictly your own affair. But you'd better be able to prove it. So far all I have heard are unsubstantiated accusations."

"I think," said the grey sleuth calmly, "my colleague has made a rather clear and concise explanation of your motives."

"*Motives?*" uttered Ronald defiantly. "Just because I may have what seems motive to kill someone doesn't prove I would…or did. You should know that better than anybody."

DeKok rubbed his hands over his craggy face. Staaten was right. There was no proof. Motive alone was not enough for a trial. With just motives, the judge advocate would not even think of prosecuting.

He closed his eyes momentarily. He felt drained and exhausted. His feet started to hurt, always a bad sign. It happened when a case was not progressing. As DeKok seemed to get farther and farther away from a solution, his feet would hurt. Sighing deeply, he slid down deeper in his chair and placed his feet on the table. With a painful grimace on his face he looked at young Staaten. He did not like the arrogance of this young man. The way in which he spoke about Nanette was cold, emotionless, without a grain of compassion for the victim. The death of the girl had not upset him in the least.

Again DeKok looked at the handsome, somewhat-weak face. He saw suspicion.

"You didn't kill Nanette?"

"No, I did *not* kill Nanette."

"You are not in any way responsible for her death?"

"It has nothing to do with me."

Slowly DeKok nodded.

"Excellent," he said resignedly, "really excellent. I like to meet innocent people." It sounded solemn. He made a tired gesture. "So there's no reason to hold anything back. You can answer *my* questions frankly and truthfully."

Ronald looked suspiciously at the old detective. He saw a tired man with the friendly face of a good-natured boxer.

"Yes," he answered. He did not sound convinced. He added, "Yes, I suppose I can."

"Then I would like to repeat my partner's question: Why did you sell the painting of Nanette?"

Staaten's eyes narrowed. Obviously he was still disturbed by the question. His reaction did not escape DeKok. He watched a shudder go through the boy's body. Ronald became white around the nose. He did not answer.

DeKok took his legs off the table. The drained, disabling feeling had disappeared. His gaze rested on the young man.

"Well?" he pressed.

Staaten swallowed. "The painting irritated me."

"Why?"

Ronald lowered his head. He seemed to wrestle with an answer. His nervous, searching fingers moved toward his dry lips.

"Because...because of the setting."

"The setting?"

Suddenly Staaten jumped out of his chair.

"Yes," his voice rose, "the setting!"

He had lost control. All his arrogance, his self-assurance were gone. His face was red and distorted. His lower lip trembled. Tears appeared in his eyes.

"The bastard!" he exclaimed intensely. "The dirty, sneaky, filthy fiend." The words tumbled out. "He made her pose on the sofa naked. You understand? He had her pose on the sofa where my mother used to rest, especially when she became ill. He just had to paint his naked slut on it. Even after her death he had to humiliate my mother."

DeKok looked at him, incredulity on his face.

"Did he do that on purpose?"

Ronald nodded emphatically.

"Yes, just to provoke me by besmirching the memory of my mother. He made it cheap, tawdry." He ground his teeth. A hint of insanity was visible in the hard green eyes. "I would have killed her," he hissed. "Oh, yes, you can be sure of that. I would have murdered her. Nanette was never going to take my mother's place. Never!" His voice rose to a fevered pitch. He screamed, "Never! Never! Never!"

16

Ronald Staaten sobbed in sorrow and regret. The noise reverberated through the small interrogation room. His head was resting on his arms, hiding his face. Long, deep sobs racked his body. Sometimes he shrieked a long wail.

DeKok stood and watched him without emotion. From his height he looked down at the shaking back of the young man in the deep-purple jacket. He wondered if Ronald was guilty.

He had seen many, many murderers during his long and varied career. He'd seen all forms, from cold stranglers to emotional, hypertense shooters. He had never been able to find anything common in killers. DeKok had known men who murdered for a few bucks, without thought or pity. He had known people who had been forced to kill in self-defense or for some other compelling reason. Judged guiltless they became guilt-ridden, constantly tortured by what they had done. What Inspector DeKok knew for certain was lions and tigers can turn out to be meek sheep, and meek sheep can turn into ruthless killers.

Further, DeKok had concluded that anybody—no matter who—was capable of murder. Perhaps, he mused, it was no more than a game of chance consisting of facts, circumstances, and emotions. If fate stacked the deck in a certain way, murder could result. It did not matter who the players were. It was only a matter of degree.

DeKok pressed his lips together. What were the murder factors for Ronald Staaten? Thoughtfully he let them pass in review. Ronald is the only son of wealthy parents. His mother and sole anchor dies early. His father, a man with a somewhat checkered sexual past and an inflated ego, wants to remarry. The boy's intense emotional bond with his mother develops into hatred toward his father. The father poses his very young love, Nanette, on the family sofa for a nude portrait. DeKok rubbed his face. It was all there.

He placed his hand on the head of the sobbing young man.

"Come," he said in a compelling, fatherly tone, "let's talk about it some more, earnestly, man to man. Murder is worth discussing."

Slowly Staaten lifted his head.

DeKok looked in the teary face. Strangely enough he felt no pity, no compassion. The sorrow, the regret of the young man left him untouched. He did not care for crying men. They irked him. He took a clean handkerchief from his pocket and tossed it at Ronald.

"Here," he said gruffly, "clean your face."

He watched while the younger man wiped the tears from his eyes. DeKok left the interrogation room and returned a few minutes later with two steaming mugs of coffee. He placed one mug in front of Staaten and started to slurp comfortably himself. Slowly the young man brought himself under control. He became calmer.

"What I don't understand," he said, "is why you didn't protest against the use of the sofa *before* the painting was done."

Staaten sipped his coffee carefully.

"I did not know."

"Didn't know what?"

"I had no idea what kind of painting it was going to be. One day Pierre Popko came to get the sofa—"

"Who's Pierre Popko?" interrupted DeKok.

"Popko is the artist who painted the portrait."

"Right. Go on."

"I said, 'Pierre, what do you want with Mother's sofa?' and he told me it was for a painting commissioned by my father. He did not tell me any more, and I did not ask. You see, I did not know Pierre planned to pose Nanette naked on it."

"Did you know Nanette at that time?"

"Yes, I did. She had come to our house several times by then. It was about a month after Pierre introduced us to her."

Surprised, DeKok stared at him.

"Nanette was introduced to you and your father by this Pierre Popko?"

Ronald nodded.

"In addition to his other activities," he said with a down-turned mouth, "Father is also a self-proclaimed Maecenas, a guardian angel of art and artists. Pierre Popko is a protégé. My father gave him commissions, introduced him to the right people. Pierre visited us often while Mother was still alive. And one evening Nanette accompanied him."

"I thought," said DeKok, "that your father had made the acquaintance of the lady through his interest in, eh, botanical subjects."

"Oh, you must have seen the rose in his lapel."

"Yes, that's what I mean."

The young man shook his head.

"You don't know Father," he said, grinning broadly. "If today he meets a young woman who cannot stand alcohol, my father will be on the wagon before the day is out. He did not start the flower routine until after he discovered Nanette worked in a flower shop."

DeKok laughed.

"Yet Nanette seemed to have made an impression on him. His marriage plans seemed in earnest."

"Father was very taken with her. Charmed is the word, I think. Certainly he had started to live in a sort of dream. The fact that a beautiful young girl was interested in him flattered his vanity, if nothing else. What would you expect?"

Staaten paused briefly, shook his head, and sighed deeply.

"Pierre Popko encouraged it. He showed my father sketches he had made of Nanette. He would praise her beauty, calling her a goddess, a reincarnated Venus, perfection personified. And the old goat listened with glowing cheeks and bated breath."

"What kind of sketches were they?"

"Just sketches. Charcoal sketches. Nude studies, of course. Nude studies of Nanette."

"Were they good? I mean, did you like them? Were they done, well, realistically?"

"They were so realistic," he grinned with disgust, "my father bought them all. Once he decided that he would marry her, he didn't want Pierre to make any more sketches of her. He did not want anybody else to have images of her. He also prohibited Nanette to pose again."

"Did Nanette obey him?"

"I don't know. *I* didn't check up on her."

DeKok looked up with sudden interest. He had detected a certain intonation in the young man's voice, a certain emphasis.

"If you didn't," he asked sharply, "who did?"

Staaten did not answer at once. He moved restlessly in his chair. Apparently he was a bit embarrassed by the question.

"Well," pressed DeKok, "who *did* check up on her?"

Ronald swallowed.

"Father, he, eh...he did not trust Pierre."

DeKok was sitting behind his desk staring soberly into the abyss of nothing. He was stuck. His progress had been slow to begin. Now there was no movement at all in the case. So far all the people he had contacted in connection with Nanette were difficult liars, or told half-truths at best. For example, Kristel must have known something about Nanette's intention to marry. Why had she not mentioned it? Barry Wielen. Without a doubt he was the mysterious tipster who led them to the painting. How and exactly what did he know about the painting? Undoubtedly Wielen knew more than he was telling.

DeKok rubbed his chin; he was thinking hard. The sheet on which he had been doodling was still on his desk. The line he had written was still there: HOW OR WHY OR THROUGH WHOM DID NANETTE DISAPPEAR? He had written that only yesterday. Really he should not be too dissatisfied with the results so far. Now, only a day later, he was able to answer part of the question. Nanette disappeared because she had been killed. Her murderer was someone who, for one reason or another, had found it necessary to mutilate the corpse in a most abhorrent manner. The last bit seemed especially important to him. Why the disfigurement? What had been the purpose?

Vledder entered the detective room. He seemed hurried and excited. He hung his wet raincoat from a peg and pushed a chair closer to DeKok's desk. His face beamed.

"Did you know," he whispered, "Nanette used to be a nurse?"

DeKok nodded slowly.

"I suspected as much," he said resignedly.

"Well, it's true. When I went to Aalsmeer to ask some questions, that's one of the things I heard. I suddenly remembered it while you were talking to Ronald Staaten. Before Nanette and Kristel started their flower shop, Nanette was a nurse, or a student nurse. I hadn't told you yet. You see, at first I didn't think it too important."

Laughing, DeKok looked at him.

"And then you thought about Brother Laurens?"

"Exactly," he exclaimed enthusiastically. "Brother Laurens! You understand, the morphine. Of course, Nanette must have gotten to know this Brother Laurens during her stint as a nurse. That seems reasonable. Somehow she got a hold over him. She coerced him into delivering drugs to her. That's the way it went, don't you think?"

"It's possible," answered the grey sleuth carefully.

Vledder's face became disappointed.

"Now what?" he asked, irked. "It *is* possible. Absolutely. It's simply obvious. As soon as we catch Brother Laurens, you'll see I'm right."

"And how do you propose to catch Brother Laurens?"

Vledder made a nonchalant gesture, suggesting that these were mere details.

"Simple. If we trace Nanette's history, her career as a nurse, then we can't help but find Brother Laurens. I've been working on it."

"And…"

"Yes, I just came from Ye Three Roses. Kristel van Daalen even has a picture of Nanette in a nurse's uniform."

Shocked, DeKok looked up.

"Did you tell her?"

"What?"

"About finding Nanette."

"No, eh, I…no, I told her nothing."

"She didn't ask?"

"No, she didn't ask anything. She just told me all about how Nanette had become a nurse, how she was interested in surgery…Kristel was really nice. So friendly she asked me to convey her regards to you."

DeKok snorted.

"How charming."

Startled, Vledder looked at him, surprised by the tone of voice.

"Is, eh, is something the matter?"

DeKok bent his head slightly and used a thumb and index finger to rub along the side of his nose toward the corners of his eyes.

"No, nothing," he said wearily. "It's all right. Go ahead. Follow the trail of Nanette's nursing career. Perhaps it *will* lead to Brother Laurens." He raised a cautioning finger. "But no further. I mean, as long as we know where to find him, that'll be enough for the moment."

"No arrest?"

"Not yet, my boy. Not yet. We still do not know enough about his activities. He's still a rather vague figure. Even the suspicion he had anything to do with Nanette or the drugs is only supposition, not fact. Just think about it."

He paused and chewed thoughtfully on his lower lip.

"Just one thing," he said pensively, "interests me to no end…"

"What?"

DeKok stared in front of him.

"Did Brother Laurens share Nanette's interest in surgery?"

The phone rang at that moment.

Vledder picked it up and listened.

"It's for you," he said, and handed the receiver to DeKok.

"Yes, DeKok here."

"You let him go," charged a familiar voice. "You let him go!" There was despair and disbelief in the voice.

"DeKok, why? You had him, you had him in your hands. All you had to do was turn the key in the lock."

"Lock up whom?"

"Young Staaten."

"And why should I do that?"

"He's the murderer. He killed Nanette Bogaard!"

DeKok sat up straight.

"What?"

"Yes. On the day Nanette disappeared, he had a date with her."

Furious, DeKok threw the receiver back on the phone.

"Who was it?" asked Vledder.

"Wielen," he answered tersely. "He came right out and stated young Staaten murdered Nanette."

"What?"

"Yes, he said he simply couldn't understand why we didn't keep Ronald. According to Wielen, the young man had a date with Nanette on the day she disappeared. He's supposed to have killed her at that time."

Vledder frowned.

"How does he know about the date?"

Dejected, DeKok shrugged his shoulders.

"He knows a lot of things. For instance, *he* was the one who called us about the painting at Mirror's Canal."

Vledder nodded agreement.

"Yes, and he was the man who wanted to buy the 'Somber Nude,' regardless of price."

"Exactly. Wielen is up to his neck in this case. And his interest is much more than just professional curiosity.

He's personally involved. He loved Nanette. Love can be the cause of the strangest situations."

DeKok narrowed his eyes to mere slits.

"But what I find so strange, what I don't understand at all is this: how does Wielen know Nanette was murdered? You see, our find at the municipal dump is not yet public knowledge. Apart from the men there and the paramedics, only the police know about the mutilated corpse."

Vledder looked at him with admiration.

"You're right. Wielen does know more than he should. That's suspicious, very suspicious."

DeKok nodded. He stood up and shuffled over to the peg above the puddle created by his dripping raincoat. He was revitalized. He started to enjoy his job again. There was progress in the case. He placed his old, ridiculous hat firmly on top of his head and struggled with the still-wet, leaky raincoat.

"Come on, my boy," he said jovially. "It's about time we present Wielen with a very apt proverb."

"A proverb?" Vledder looked dumbfounded.

"Never heard of it?" asked the old detective, grinning. "Very well known, I assure you: 'The more you know, the more you have to answer for.'" He moved toward the door.

Vledder's entire face was transformed by a wide grin.

Barry Wielen looked exhausted, as if he had not slept for days on end. His grey eyes looked dull. His face was grey. Even his remarkable mustache drooped. He stared at DeKok with a melancholy gaze.

"I expected you," he said with a deep sigh. "To tell you the truth, that's why I stayed home."

"Uncommonly accommodating."

"Nothing to do with accommodating you," answered Wielen, shaking his head. "You owe me an explanation. That's what I'm waiting for. Why did you let Ronald Staaten go? Why didn't you arrest him?" His voice sounded demanding. "You let him go," he continued, "without checking the facts or the background. That's unforgivable. You let a murderer go free."

DeKok looked at him without emotion and did not react.

Wielen became excited. He raised his voice.

"If you don't arrest Nanette's killer within twenty-four hours," he yelled, "I'll write a piece about you that will destroy your reputation forever. You hear me? You'll be ruined as a policeman. Forever! I won't leave a piece of you intact."

Not the least impressed, DeKok waited patiently until he was through. Then he rose slowly from the easy chair in which he sat. His broad face looked serious. Carefully he extended a hand toward the reporter.

"My sincere condolences," he said soberly. "I sympathize with your loss. Nanette Bogaard was the object of your love and devotion. The news of her death must have been a shock for you."

Wielen hesitated momentarily. He searched DeKok's face. He was trying to find a trace of mockery, of insincerity. He could not find it, so he took the extended hand.

"Thank you," he said hoarsely.

"I would have liked to have softened the shock for you. For instance, I would have preferred to be the one to bring you the news. But from your phone call, I understand that you had already heard."

It was both a statement and a question. Wielen nodded.

"Somebody called me."

"Who?"

The reporter made a vague gesture.

"I, eh, I've acquaintances with the police. They keep me informed of interesting case developments."

The sad, somewhat mild expression on DeKok's face changed. It turned cold, an icy mask.

"Interesting case developments?" he said biting, sardonic. "Yes, such as the discovery of the dismembered corpse of a lively young woman. A woman you knew, cared for, loved. Interesting, no doubt, especially for the press."

Wielen covered his face with his hands.

"Stop it!" he screamed. "Stop it."

DeKok snorted. His nostrils trembled.

"Nanette Bogaard. What did you call her again? Oh, yes, the 'wild daisy from Ye Three Roses.' She was a treasure! Wow-wow-wow, what a broad. And you had not seen her for at least two weeks." His voice dripped with sarcasm.

Wielen groaned. DeKok's words struck like punches. They hurt him to the quick, to the most hidden part of his soul. He dropped into a low chair. With difficulty he managed to swallow his tears.

DeKok too sat down again. His anger had receded. He had wounded the young man on purpose. It had been premeditated, to break through Wielen's resistant exterior. Comfortably he stretched his legs and looked around the room. A small porcelain vase of wildflowers stood on a bookshelf. The stems were already wilting.

"If," he said calmly, "you had been a bit more forthright with me from the beginning, if you had answered all my questions honestly, perhaps I'd know now who killed her." His tone changed, it became sharper. "All right," he continued, "you've been playing your cat-and-mouse game long enough. The time has come to lay the facts on the table." He leaned forward threateningly. "And believe me," he said harshly, "if you try to hide the smallest detail, I won't leave a piece of *you* intact."

The hint of a smile started underneath the reporter's heavy mustache.

"You're right," he sighed. "At first I didn't think it was all that serious. I was thinking in terms of an exclusive for the paper, more concerned about breaking a story than about Nanette. My thinking was wrong. You see, as I saw it, Nanette was not at all the type of girl to get into trouble. She was so independent, and stayed too...removed. Nanette was mercurial. She couldn't be pinned down by any man. She constantly slipped through one's fingers. She was not at all the type to fall into seven canals at the same time, as we say in Holland."

"You only need one canal to drown," observed DeKok.

Wielen nodded slowly.

"Indeed," he agreed somberly. "That's obvious, after the fact. She wasn't as untouchable as I thought. Somebody got ahold of her."

They remained silent for a long time. DeKok was the first to break the silence.

"But your conduct in this whole affair is not at all clear. Tell us about Nanette's visit to the Red Light District two weeks ago, and anything you know about the date she had with Ronald Staaten. It seems to me you deliberately tried to mislead the police by not telling us everything."

"I did, you're right. I loved Nanette. Her secret visits to the District intrigued me. But they remain unexplained."

DeKok grinned. His craggy face was transformed into a picture of boyish mischief.

"And thus you thought, 'This is an excellent opportunity. If I give the police a hint, then they'll solve the problem for me.' Isn't that right?"

Wielen sighed, a mixture of regret and a guilty conscience.

"It could have been a lead," he said apologetically. "It could have had something to do with her disappearance."

"Come now, you didn't believe that yourself," challenged DeKok.

"No, not really. I'm not that naïve. It seemed more of a joke, one of Nanette's bag of tricks…to get rid of Old Mealymouth."

DeKok's eyebrows were poised for one of their remarkable performances.

"Old Mealymouth?"

"That's what she called Staaten, the stockbroker."

"Why?"

"He pursued her day and night with proposals of marriage. Staaten is a rich man. He kept repeating what he could offer her, in addition to his own sweet, charming self."

"And?"

Irritated, Wielen looked up.

"What do you mean *and*?" he asked.

"What was Nanette's response?"

"Of course she didn't want anything to do with the old goat. After all, he was almost three times as old as she. He persisted. At wit's end, she finally made an appointment with Ronald. She wanted to ask him to ask his father to stop pestering her. You understand?"

"Yes, I understand," nodded DeKok. "And she made the date for the day she disappeared."

"Exactly. I saw her that day at Ye Three Roses. As you astutely noticed, I bought a bouquet of wildflowers. That's when she told me about her meeting with Ronald."

"Therefore you concluded that Ronald killed Nanette?"

"Yes, that's obvious. He was the last person to see Nanette alive. He must have killed her."

"And what about the motive?"

Wielen shrugged his shoulders.

"Perhaps," he said hesitatingly, "he was afraid his father would marry Nanette anyway."

"Against her will?"

A painful expression came over the reporter's face.

"You never know," he admitted reluctantly. "Money... money is a powerful inducement, after all."

DeKok smiled.

"Your faith in her left room for doubt?"

Wielen made a sad gesture.

"Nanette was, after all, a woman." He seemed to think it explained everything.

DeKok took a closer look at the young man. In his heart he felt a mild affection, a bit of empathy. It was as if he discovered something of himself in the journalist, a similar way of looking at things. After a while he said, "Tell me about the painting." His voice was friendly.

"The nude?"

"Indeed, the nude on the red sofa," he nodded.

"Nanette," Wielen answered lazily, "used to work as a model. It was a way for her to earn extra pocket money. I was against it." He made a helpless gesture. "But what could I do? After all, I had no authority over her. As far as friendly influence is concerned, she was someone who simply could not be told what to do." He sighed deeply. "She did what she wanted," he continued. "Pierre Popko, her favorite artist, painted her nude. It was an extremely good painting, striking. I saw it just after it was finished."

"Where?"

"We were in his studio on Prince's Island. I used to pick Nanette up from time to time when she was modeling."

"And?"

"I think Nanette raised the subject with old Staaten somehow. In any case he bought the painting from Popko and gave it a home in his living room. Personally it made me furious when I heard about it. What the hell did Mealymouth want with a nude Nanette on his wall? One day, in a rash mood, I went to Staaten. I'd had a few, and bluntly made him an offer for the painting. I didn't have all that much money, but believe me, I would have spent every last cent to get that painting."

A faint smile was visible behind the moustache.

"Staaten gave me a cold look, like a dead cod. He laughed in my face. He called me a poor local hack. He showed me all his paintings, rubbing my nose in his wealth. I wanted to punch him in his fat, rich face...but I missed. I think I must have had more to drink than I thought."

He paused again.

"Last night, rather late," he continued, "I was hanging around in the Emperor's Canal neighborhood."

"Near the Staaten residence?"

"Yes. I knew she, Nanette, had a date with Ronald the night before. I was hoping to catch a glimpse of her, to discover her whereabouts. It would have made a nice headline for the paper, 'Reporter Finds Missing Girl.'"

"But there was no headline," grinned DeKok.

"No," he sighed again. "No, it didn't result in anything. I didn't see Nanette. All I saw was the elder Staaten coming home around eleven thirty. At last I gave up and went home to sleep. I thought Nanette would undoubtedly resurface. On the way home I walked along the quiet side of Mirror's Canal. I go there often. I like antiques, and I like to hunt around the old stores."

"That's when you discovered the painting?"

"Yes, I couldn't believe my eyes. It didn't make sense. My first thought was I *had* to have that painting. This was my chance, you see. I went to the nearest phone, rang the owner, and asked him to keep the painting for me. He asked for my name, and I gave it to him."

He paused, searched for a cigarette, but did not light it.

"As I walked back along Mirror's Canal to take a good look at the painting once more, I thought how strange it was for Staaten to have suddenly sold the painting. Something must have happened to change his mind. Maybe he felt he had to get rid of the painting, get her memory out of the house."

He played with the cigarette, picking at it absentmindedly.

"After a while I figured the best thing to do was to ask him. Why not? I went back to the phone booth, called him, and asked why he had sold *Nanette*."

He dropped the demolished cigarette in an ashtray.

"Staaten wasn't even surprised," he continued. "He told me the painting had been stolen from his house. He had discovered the theft only ten minutes earlier. So I told him where he could find it."

DeKok nodded slowly.

"And," he said grinning somberly, "after you had told everybody, contacted everyone you could think to alert, you decided to give the vaguest possible hint to the police. It was a sort of afterthought, just a little puzzle piece to keep the boys occupied."

Wielen bowed his head.

17

"Do you think Wielen will keep his word? Will he withhold the news of Nanette's murder? What about his paper? It is, after all, news," remarked Vledder.

They were walking through the inner city on their way back from Wielen's house to Warmoes Street. It was still raining. The wet asphalt mirrored the garish lights of neon advertising.

DeKok pulled up the collar of his raincoat a little higher and shoved his hat a little deeper down over his ears.

"In exchange," he growled, "I promised him the exclusive. As soon as we unveil who killed Nanette, he'll be the first to know."

"But why are you so insistent that the report of her death be kept out of the papers? After all, there are already enough people who know."

"Brother Laurens?"

Vledder shrugged his shoulders. "If he's the killer, he doesn't need to read it in the papers."

"Exactly. I'm interested in what Laurens does and doesn't know. Does he already know about her death? If so, how?"

"Do you consider him a suspect?"

DeKok sighed, avoiding a puddle.

"Well, not more or less than anyone else with a reasonable motive."

"Such as?"

"Broker Staaten."

He spoke the name so lightly, almost as an afterthought, that Vledder slowed his step.

"Staaten Senior?"

Slowly DeKok nodded agreement.

Suddenly it started to rain harder, a veritable downpour. They were in the middle of the Dam. Vledder ran from the open square to the nearest shelter. On the corner of one of the streets he fled into The Red Lion. He stood panting in the lobby. DeKok approached at speed using his strange waddling gait. Vledder laughed. DeKok at top speed was always a comic sight.

They stood in the lobby for a while and watched the rain fall. Everybody seemed to have been swept from the streets by the sudden torrents of water.

DeKok shook his hat more or less dry and wiped his face with a handkerchief. Then he took Vledder by the arm.

"Come, my boy," he said shakily, "I need something against the chill in my bones. I'll treat you to coffee and cognac."

Together they entered through the revolving door.

There were only few people in the bar. The detectives hung their wet coats on a peg and found a free table near the window.

A waiter delivered their order silently.

When the man disappeared, Vledder said, "You didn't really mean it, did you, when you said that old man Staaten had a motive for killing Nanette?"

DeKok did not answer. With obvious pleasure he sipped his coffee laced with cognac.

"Have a drink first," he said jovially, "it'll do you good. People in our job need a bracer like this now and then."

"But Staaten wanted to marry her. Why would he kill the woman he was planning to marry?"

DeKok took a big swallow from his coffee.

"Maybe it was revenge; she injured his vanity. If you listened carefully to Wielen's story, you'll recall Nanette wasn't too flattering when she spoke about Staaten. She ridiculed him, called him 'Old Mealymouth.' That shows a remarkable lack of respect for one's future husband."

DeKok remained silent for a while, contemplating the weather outside.

"Just imagine," he then said pontifically, "Nanette had indeed agreed to marry Staaten. Later he found out, one way or another, the girl didn't care for him at all. It wasn't enough she ran around and cheated on him, she ridiculed him to others. It's certainly motive for a crime of passion."

Vledder looked at his mentor with admiration. "Indeed, you're right. I hadn't thought of that possibility." He chewed thoughtfully on his lower lip. "But let's say your reasoning is correct. With whom did Nanette cheat? Wielen? From the conversations we've had so far, that seems hardly a viable relationship."

DeKok shook his head.

"Not Wielen, but Pierre Popko."

Vledder looked surprised.

"Who's Pierre Popko?"

"He is the artist who painted the 'Somber Nude.' Ronald told me about him. He also told me his father used to check up on Nanette."

"Check up on her? Why?"

Again DeKok shook his head.

"You see, as soon as the broker decided that he was going to marry Nanette, he didn't want her to model any longer. Specifically he didn't want her to model for Popko. He didn't trust the painter."

Vledder's eyes sparkled.

"But that's beautiful," he exclaimed, "just beautiful. Then we *have* solved the case after all. Broker Staaten found out that Nanette was cheating on him. He became angry and killed her."

DeKok raised his hands in a repudiating gesture.

"Ho, ho," he said laughing, "it's not that simple. You're much too hasty. You neglect, undoubtedly due to youthful exuberance, a few facts. Just think—"

Suddenly he stopped in mid-sentence. His grey eyes filled with a strange expression, a bit jumpy. He looked past Vledder.

"Don't turn around," he said hoarsely. "Kristel van Daalen is behind you. She's just coming through the door. She's with a man, a tall guy with a beard."

They were outside on the Dam, walking again. It was still raining, but the heavy rain had stopped. People passed by toting umbrellas.

Vledder pulled an injured face.

"Was that really necessary?" he asked moodily. "Was it? Dammit! Even if she had seen us, so what? It's Saturday night, you know. Look around, people do go out. There's certainly nothing strange about Kristel going out with a friend, even a tall friend with a beard. So what?" He snorted audibly, displaying utter contempt. Then, unable to leave it alone, he continued, "You're always looking for a hidden motive. You're being ridiculous, suspicious of everything. Here we are slinking away like thieves in the night, just because you don't want Kristel to see us. How idiotic—I'm surprised you took the time to pay the check."

DeKok whistled a Christmas song through his teeth. He always whistled Christmas songs when he whistled, regardless of the season. Vledder's protests rolled off his back. He knew exactly what bothered his pupil. The boy was thinking of Celine, of course, his girlfriend. It was Saturday night, and he was missing his girl. But as long as the Nanette case was unresolved...

Suddenly he stopped in the middle of the street and looked at his watch. It was past nine o'clock.

"I think you should go see her, my boy," he said in a fatherly tone. "I bet she's waiting for you, am I right?"

Vledder looked suspiciously at the face of his mentor. It seemed DeKok could read his thoughts. It was downright spooky.

He swallowed. "I, um, I...think so, yes."

DeKok nodded his encouragement.

"The autopsy has been scheduled for tomorrow at ten. Please make sure that, at the very least, you're there in time to meet Doctor Rusteloos. I'll see you at the station afterward." He gestured. "If I'm not there, the desk sergeant will know how to reach me."

He patted his pupil on the shoulder.

"Give her my best," he said in farewell.

Hesitating, Vledder stood his ground.

"And you," he asked dubiously, "what are you going to do?"

"I'm going to try to get ahold of Ronald Staaten before the night is out."

"Ronald Staaten?"

"Yes."

"Why?"

DeKok smiled gently.

"Very simple. To ask him how his Thursday evening date with Nanette went."

"Are you home alone?"

"No, Father is home too. Come in."

Ronald Staaten led the way. DeKok followed him along the long marble corridor. Their footsteps sounded hollow echoing against the high walls. A wide staircase at the end of the corridor led upstairs.

"Father will be surprised."

"How's that?"

"I don't think he expected visitors."

"Ah, but my visit has to do with you, not your father."

"With me?" Surprised, Ronald turned around.

"But if your father is home anyway," nodded DeKok, "it might be a good idea for him to be present when we have our little talk. Perhaps we can eliminate a number of misunderstandings."

They climbed the wide marble stairs. At the top, mounted on a black granite pedestal, DeKok saw a bronze statue of Mercury. This was a scaled-down replica of Mercury, the god of trade, from atop the stock exchange.

Ronald stopped in front of a high carved door. He hesitated. It was as if he had to steel himself against something. It lasted only an instant. Composed, he opened the door and entered.

"Father," he announced, "here's Inspector DeKok."

The broker rose from a large easy chair with a high back. He looked at ease and relaxed, half-glasses perched on the end of his nose. He was dressed in a wrinkled robe, with felt slippers on his feet. He looked the opposite of the dapper man-about-town.

"With a kay-oh-kay," Staaten smiled.

DeKok nodded.

"Indeed, you remembered."

Again Staaten smiled politely.

"Please sit down," he said with an expansive gesture. "To what do we owe the honor of your visit? Would you like something to drink? A sherry, or would you prefer something else?"

"Cognac, please."

"Ronald," the voice sounded dominating, authoritative.

"Yes, Father."

Young Staaten complied immediately. He went to an intricately carved oak buffet and returned with a sparkling cognac glass and a bottle of old French cognac.

DeKok recognized the label.

Ronald looked a question at him.

"Would you like me to warm the glass?"

DeKok shook his head.

"No need, it'll warm in my hand."

"As you like."

It sounded shy, almost scared.

DeKok's eyebrows contracted, rippled briefly. This was a far cry from the Ronald Staaten he knew, not at all the young man who had reacted with such spontaneous passion. The arrogant attitude had vanished. Under the penetrating eyes of his father he behaved in a nervous manner. He was as humble as a servant in his father's household. DeKok closed his eyes and saw Ronald as a marionette doll. A thousand invisible strings held him under the stern will of the man in felt slippers.

Ronald poured.

DeKok rocked the glass in his hand and inhaled the stimulating aroma of the drink. Meanwhile his gaze roamed the room. It was tastefully decorated. Although the room was large, almost a small ballroom, it was sparingly furnished. There was a certain atmosphere of intimacy, warmth. It was quite comfortable.

The walls were almost completely covered with paintings of different sizes. Most were portraits, figurative paintings. As a sort of concession to the strict figurative realism of most of the paintings, he discovered two smaller works by Renoir and a number of canvasses by lesser-known French impressionists.

There were no gaps apparent. The place that had once been occupied by the 'Somber Nude' had been filled again.

The elder Staaten watched DeKok closely.

"You're interested in paintings?"

DeKok sipped from his cognac.

"In general no, paintings in general do not interest me. Only sometimes, if a painting is able to awaken certain emotions. If it appeals to my sense of life, then and only then will I be tempted to take a closer look, to study it."

Staaten smiled.

"You're entitled to your opinion. Don't you think, Ronald, it's an interesting point of view?"

The young man had seated himself in an easy chair. His legs were elegantly crossed, the fingertips of his slender hands pressed together.

"Yes, Father," he answered softly, "it is an interesting point of view."

He repeated it monotone, almost mechanically. DeKok looked at both men. Father and son were clearly opposites. Nanette Bogaard had entered into both their lives. She was beautiful, frivolous, fun loving, and, without a doubt, a little cruel.

DeKok placed his glass on a low table and gestured.

"For instance, the nude on the red sofa touched me as few portraits ever have. Even had I not been involved in this case, I would have been struck by the painting. It fascinated me from the first time I saw it. There is an intense sadness in the subject's eyes. The impression created by the nude body contributes to the somber effect. It is as though the woman is without life. The sterile treatment removes any sexual temptation or overtones. It was as if the painter subconsciously detected an aura of approaching doom surrounding his model. He faithfully recorded the shadow of approaching disaster. There is a veil of death over the painting."

A long silence ensued. When he finished speaking, DeKok's words hung in the air. They mingled with the rushing of the rain outside. An English pendulum clock on the mantelpiece ticked away an eternity.

Ronald looked pale. His hands shook. The elder Staaten moved his feet. He was the first to break the silence.

"Pierre Popko," he said in a hoarse voice, "is a gifted painter, without a doubt. But I would not go so far as to say he has paranormal powers—he is no psychic. I believe, Mr. DeKok, you may have been influenced by your rich imagination. You definitely saw more in the painting than there possibly could have been."

DeKok gave him a winning smile.

"But Nanette is dead, is she not?"

Staaten nodded.

"Ronald told me. I believe you hinted as much during his interrogation."

"Yes, indeed, she was murdered in a most horrible way. I'll spare you the details. That is…" he paused for effect, "…unless you're already familiar with them."

It took a while before the poison had its effect. Then Staaten jumped up. His fingers writhed as if wanting to strangle something. His eyes flashed.

"What are you trying to say?"

Every fiber of DeKok's body was tense. Just this morning he had bared witness to the unexpected strength of the broker. He remembered the painful streaks on Vledder's neck.

He pointed at Ronald. "Your son," he said accusingly, "had a date with Nanette on the day she disappeared. She's not been seen alive since."

Staaten's face became a mask. He looked from DeKok to his son, his glance darting back and forth.

"Ronald?"

The young man started to tremble under his father's intense stare. He nodded almost imperceptibly. His mouth opened, but no sound came forth.

For just a moment DeKok feared that Staaten was about to hit his son. But the broker controlled himself.

"You...you had a date with Nanette?"

"Yes, Father."

"Behind my back?"

Suddenly something seemed to snap in the young man. It seemed to DeKok he finally broke away from the thousands of ties connecting him to the will of his father. He stopped being a puppet on a string. Even his body language changed. Firmly he looked his father straight in the eyes.

"Yes," he exclaimed sharply, "behind your back! One day I went to Ye Three Roses and told Nanette I needed to see her, talk to her alone. I wouldn't have felt at ease in your presence. That's what I told her. I also told her it really was my right to discuss certain things with her if, eh, if she was going to be my mother. She refused at first, laughed at me, but finally promised to see me."

DeKok intervened.

"So you made a date with Nanette and not the other way around? I mean, you took the initiative?"

Ronald looked at him with surprise.

"Yes, I—"

"Where was she going?"

"You mean, where were we supposed to meet?"

"Yes."

"Here, in this house."

"What did you want to discuss with her?"

The young man started to grin. The result was a strange, joyless grimace.

"I...I didn't have anything to discuss with her. I just wanted to kill her...kill...kill..."

He kept repeating it in a hypnotic cadence.

The elder Staaten gripped his son by the shoulders and shook him violently.

"Shut your mouth," he hissed. "Shut your mouth!"

Ronald hardly noticed him.

"But she didn't come," he said, wagging his head. "No, she never came, didn't come at all, she didn't..."

An idiotic smile played around his lips.

The elder Staaten let go of his son and turned to DeKok.

"When was he supposed to meet her?"

"Thursday evening."

For a few moments the broker remained motionless, standing between his son and the inspector. DeKok saw him think fast. In seconds he inspected, rejected, and considered a number of factors. Then he sat down and sighed.

"My son," he said formally, "did not murder Nanette. I can testify to that. I was with him all evening."

18

"What did Doctor Rusteloos have to say?"

Vledder grinned. "He complained that we always need him during the weekend. He wanted to know if the police were aware that there are other days in the week. Or did they only know about Saturday and Sunday?"

"So we caught him in a bad mood?" asked DeKok, laughing.

"No. I've actually never really seen him in a bad mood. He knows it isn't our fault."

"And the autopsy?"

Vledder grimaced, showing disgust.

"I'll never get used to it. It was unusually gruesome this time. All those separate parts…"

"What did the doctor say about the mutilation?"

Vledder took out his notebook.

"I wrote it down for you. It was rather interesting. Just a moment, here it is: *The amputations were performed with a certain amount of professionalism. The perpetrator—as evidenced by the condition of the skeleton, the placement of the cuts in relation to the direction of muscle and attachment of tendons—must have been possessed of more than the usual amount of anatomical knowledge.*"

He closed the notebook with a slap.

"What do you think of that?"

DeKok made a vague movement with his shoulders; it was not quite a shrug.

"What do you want me to think about it?"

Vledder sighed heavily.

"Just think about Brother Laurens," he cried, irritated by DeKok's apparent obtuseness. "What do you think about his 'anatomical knowledge'? Nurses are sometimes almost as knowledgeable as doctors."

DeKok nodded slowly.

"What did the good doctor say about the cause of death?"

Vledder was offended by the scant interest DeKok seemed to display.

"Strangulation," he said grudgingly.

"Strangled?"

"Yes."

"How?"

"The murderer used a scarf or a nylon stocking. It could have been done by hand, but because of the mutilation that was less easily established. Doctor Rusteloos was convinced, however, that the young woman was strangled first. The amputations happened later."

"How much later?"

"Perhaps several hours, according to the doctor."

"Were there traces of a fight, a struggle?"

Vledder shook his head.

"There were no indications of that. No visible damage to the skin, no subcutaneous bleeding or bruising."

"Loss of urine?"

"Probably not, there was still urine in the bladder."

DeKok nodded thoughtfully.

"Excellent," he said, "really excellent. Did you ask the doctor, in view of possible drug abuse, to look out for puncture marks?"

Vledder grimaced.

"If you wanted to know all that, I would have thought you'd go to the autopsy yourself."

Amazed, DeKok looked at him.

"But why? I have an excellent assistant."

Vledder showed the beginning of a smile.

"There were no puncture marks," he said with in affected voice, "that is to say, no recent puncture marks on the skin indicating drug use. Of course, a toxicological investigation has not yet been completed. Satisfied?"

"More than content," laughed DeKok.

Vledder pushed his chair closer to DeKok's desk and sat down comfortably.

"I'm always glad when such an autopsy is behind me. How did it go last night? Did you get ahold of Ronald?"

"Yes."

"And?"

"He admitted he had made a date with Nanette. He waited for her all night Thursday evening, but Nanette did not show up."

Vledder grinned.

"That's easy to say."

"Indeed, but his father provided an airtight alibi. He says he can testify that Ronald didn't kill Nanette. He was with Ronald all Thursday evening."

Vledder frowned, a deep crease on his forehead.

"So," he said hesitatingly, "those two provide each other's alibis—difficult to break."

DeKok rubbed his hands over his face.

"Father and son," he said pensively, "united, perhaps for the first time in their lives."

He stared a bit dreamily at nothing at all. His elbows rested on his desk, his hands under the chin. He stared at a lost fly that tripped across his desk blotter. It stopped from time to time and rubbed its front legs together. He followed the movements of the fly subconsciously. When it finally flew away, he rose with some difficulty. He walked over to a closet and took something out. Then he shuffled over to the peg where he kept his raincoat.

"When you have recovered sufficiently from the autopsy," he said, lightly mocking, "I think I'd like to hit the road again."

"Hit the road? Where do you want to go?"

"Amsterdam West, Ox Village. They've got an apartment building there, Woodwind or Wood House…"

He fished a crumpled piece of paper from his pocket and looked at some chicken scratches.

"Oh, it's Wood's Edge."

Vledder's face showed complete incomprehension.

"Wood's Edge?"

DeKok grinned broadly. It was his most endearing expression.

"While you were at the autopsy I wasn't exactly doing nothing, you know. I had a long visit at the city registrar's office."

"On a Sunday? It's closed, isn't it?"

DeKok nodded.

"Yes, but I found a Mr. Slosser prepared to sacrifice a few hours of his Sunday to help me look up a number of things."

Confused, Vledder looked at his mentor.

"Things, what sort of things?"

"If you had been thinking clearly," said DeKok, mildly reproachful, "you wouldn't have had to ask that question. You would have known. In any case, Wood's Edge was the result. And that's where we're going."

Vledder followed his mentor from the room with his head low, a bit glum after the correction. He thought about the how and wherefore.

Suddenly he saw something hanging from DeKok's hand. It was the old doll with the fixed smile and the missing leg, the one DeKok had picked up at the city dump.

"What do you want with that dirty thing?"

The question had been asked too quickly. Vledder realized immediately he should have thought about it first. Everything DeKok does has a purpose. The doll, too, must serve a purpose.

DeKok turned around slowly and looked at Vledder. An almost sad expression was in his eyes.

"You still don't understand, do you?"

Soberly Vledder shook his head.

"No," he said timidly, "I have to confess."

The old inspector smiled.

"Just come along, my boy," he said jovially. "I'll explain everything. I promise."

Wood's Edge in Ox Village was the outermost of a series of inviting apartment buildings placed in an L shape among abundant greenery. Eight stories high, centrally heated and cooled, the building featured spacious elevators and more than a hundred similarly shaped units per building. Each apartment had a large living room, two bedrooms, kitchen, lobby, and bathroom. The individual entrances were located along spacious galleries. It was a development typical of Northern Europe. The development was reminiscent of long rows of townhouses, one on top of another, a wide gallery in front of each house instead of a street.

Vledder parked the VW Beetle behind the building. DeKok got out of the car, doll in one hand. Vledder closed the car and followed him. Together they approached the entrance.

In front of the elevators DeKok halted and took the crumpled piece of paper out of his pocket. He showed Vledder a row of numbers.

"These are the numbers," he explained, "of the units in which live families with children, girls. I excluded units of families with just boys."

"You got that from the registrar's office?"

DeKok nodded.

"First I want to make sure that Wood's Edge is the right building."

"Oh!"

"You see, an old doll has certain characteristics. Like any well-loved toy, it develops its own individuality after a time."

He shook his head and looked almost tenderly at the fixed smile of the doll.

In the round porthole of the shaft, the light of a descending elevator became visible. The doors hissed open and a number of men, women, and children emerged.

A boy of about eight looked at DeKok and the doll in his hand while passing. He walked on for a few paces. Then he stood stock still, turned, and came back hesitatingly. Before DeKok could enter the elevator, he spoke. "Where did you find the doll, mister?"

The inspector looked down at the boy. The little guy looked neat and well cared for. He wore grey slacks, a blue blazer with brass buttons, and a baseball cap.

"Why?"

"That's my little sister's doll."

"So, well, well." He was shaken by the sudden success. "You see," he continued after a moment, "I would like to return the doll to your mother. I'm looking for her. Of course, I don't know in which flat you live."

The boy laughed politely.

"Ninety-three, mister. You want me to show you the way? It's on the third gallery."

"Yes, please."

They entered the elevator. The boy ran ahead on the third gallery. He left the front door of unit ninety-three open.

"Mother, Mother," they heard him call, "there's a man outside, and he's got Elly's doll."

It took a few moments. Then a young woman appeared in the door opening. DeKok estimated her to be in her early thirties. She looked attractive, fresh, in a flowery summer dress. She looked from DeKok to

Vledder. The look was full of suspicion. A small blush of excitement was on her cheeks.

DeKok smiled his best smile. It was not as good as his grin, but still very winning.

"This is Elly's doll, I understand?"

"Yes, that's Bibette," nodded the woman.

"Who?"

"Bibette, that's what my daughter calls the doll. She is rather wild with it. You have to watch her all the time—given half a chance and an open window, she throws the doll out of the window. You found the old thing in the street, I imagine. To tell the truth, I haven't seen it for a few days now."

"Since when? Can you remember?"

Her face took on a pensive expression.

"Let's see...I think Thursday, yes, it had to be Thursday. She was still playing with it then."

DeKok nodded encouragement.

"Excellent, really excellent." He handed her the doll. "Well, here's Bibette again. Home, safe and sound."

The woman accepted the doll and looked at it carefully.

"Where did you find it?"

DeKok hesitated. He did not want to answer that question. A bit reticent, he scratched the back of his neck.

"At the city dump, near Canal F."

"At the dump?"

"Indeed."

The young woman looked at him. An expression of astonishment mingled with disbelief on her face.

She dropped the doll and smoothed her dress with both hands.

"H-how?" she spluttered. "How did the doll wind up there? And how did you…"

DeKok raised a restraining hand.

"Perhaps," he said gently, "I'll tell you, one of these days. Just one observation: Watch more than just open windows when your daughter is playing with her doll. Also watch the flap of the garbage chute in the kitchen."

He bowed in farewell.

The woman looked after them as they walked down the gallery.

"Next time," she called, "please come when my husband is home."

DeKok waved.

"Prudes," he snarled, "here in Wood's Edge."

Vledder grinned at his mentor.

"You're losing your touch. You've lost your charm, that's what it is. Besides, I wonder how your wife would have reacted if two guys suddenly appeared on her front door with a dirty old doll that they found in the garbage."

DeKok did not answer.

He looked diagonally up at the numbering of the units. It took his complete attention. The last unit on the third gallery was number 105. Beyond that the gallery ended with a bank of elevators.

"If I'm right," he murmured, "we'll find one hundred and twenty-three just above ninety-three." He spoke more to himself than to Vledder. "I'm almost certain," he concluded.

Vledder shrugged his shoulders.

"Suppose you tell me first what we're after. Perhaps I can help."

"Yes, of course," DeKok nodded absentmindedly.

When the elevator appeared they entered and went to the next floor up. Again they walked along a gallery, DeKok in front. Suddenly he halted and Vledder read 123.

"This is where you wanted to go?"

"Yes."

"There's no name on the door."

"No."

"Who lives here?"

Vledder became a little excited. The blood rushed to his head. DeKok's mysterious behavior started to fray his nerves.

"Dammit," he yelled, "say something! What are you wanting to do?"

Preoccupied, DeKok looked up.

"What do I want? I want to go inside."

Vledder sighed.

"I don't think anyone is home. Just look, all the curtains are closed."

"I figured on that, more or less," DeKok grinned.

Carefully he looked along the gallery. When he saw nobody in sight, he took a small steel instrument from his pocket and used it to attack the lock.

Vledder looked shocked.

"Y-you can't do that," he stuttered. "If the occupant complains…"

"I don't think he will."

Carefully probing with the sensitive tips of his fingers, the grey sleuth worried the lock.

DeKok was extremely experienced in the opening of diverse types of locks. He knew all about beards and shanks, cylinders and tumblers. Years ago he had followed a personal course of instruction with a friend, a burglar, Handy Henkie. Henkie decided to follow the narrow but honest path of righteousness. So he turned his complete instrumentarium over to DeKok. It was a melancholy offering on the altar of virtue. DeKok used it discreetly on certain occasions.

Suddenly the door of the flat opened. He motioned for Vledder to follow him. Together they entered, and carefully DeKok closed the door behind them.

Softly on tiptoe they slunk forward through the small foyer.

The foyer opened onto a largish living room. The light was diffused, penetrating only marginally through the closed curtains. But it was enough to make out their surroundings.

A combination sofa was placed roughly in the middle of the room. It was a large, pompous piece of furniture consisting mainly of ribbed velvet and chrome. Nearby, closer to the window, was a large standing lamp. A few cheap paintings, the kind bought at roadside stalls, covered the walls. To the left they saw an ugly green vase filled with dried cornstalks on a bare sideboard. The interior was cold and sterile; it was doubtful a woman with a caring hand had ever entered the flat.

Vledder touched DeKok's elbow.

"What are we looking for?" he whispered.

DeKok shrugged.

"Just look around," he whispered back. "Be careful not to touch anything. Leave things as they are."

"Okay, boss."

DeKok gave his pupil a crushing look. He didn't like to be called "boss," and the combination of "okay" and "boss" got him. Hands in his pockets, he entered the kitchen. There, too, the curtains were closed. This was remarkable in a country where people prided themselves on the interiors of their homes. In Holland, people seldom close their curtains, except in their bedrooms. DeKok's experienced eye, trained to see every detail, inspected the surroundings. He took a lot of time looking at the knives.

Suddenly he heard a muffled cry. Vledder, shock and disbelief on his face, came out of a bedroom.

"What's the matter?"

Vledder swallowed, trying to control himself.

"In the bedroom," he panted hoarsely.

"What?"

"Nanette's clothes."

19

Spread out on the bed were a dark blue skirt with matching jacket, a white lace blouse, a nylon slip bordered with lace, a garter belt, and a minimal brassiere. Next to the bed, over the back of a chair, were a pair of nylon stockings and a pair of black underwear with "Wednesday" embroidered on them. A pair of blue-and-white pumps were placed neatly under the chair.

For a long while the detectives looked at the tableau.

"Did you see," whispered Vledder, "that it says 'Wednesday' on the panties?"

"Yes."

"But she disappeared on Thursday."

DeKok sighed.

"It doesn't mean a thing. She was still alive on Thursday. That's certain. In addition to Kristel's testimony, we also know that from Barry Wielen's story. He visited her that Thursday at Ye Three Roses. Besides, you may remember I asked you once about underwear with the names of the days."

"I was thinking about something completely different then," nodded Vledder.

DeKok ignored the remark. He leaned over the bed. A few long blonde hairs sparkled against the dark blue of the jacket. He looked at them carefully but left them untouched. Then he walked around the bed and took one of the nylon stockings from the chair and went to the window. Carefully he pushed the curtains aside and in the brighter light looked at the fine mesh of the stocking. Vledder came closer.

"You see something?"

DeKok shook his head.

"No ladders. The rest of the clothing too seems undamaged and spotless."

"And?"

"It can mean one of two things. Either Nanette undressed herself, or the one who undressed her had plenty of time to do it. I don't know if you have ever tried to take off a woman's clothes..." He looked preoccupiedly at Vledder and sighed again. "Never mind, forget it," he added.

He walked away from the window and placed the stocking over the back of the chair again. Then he looked thoughtfully around.

"A purse is missing, I think, and some form of outer clothing. Women almost always carry some sort of purse. As far as rain gear is concerned, it rained buckets last Thursday."

He rubbed his hand over his grey hair.

"I'm sure there's a raincoat around here somewhere. But I also think we better not touch anything else for the moment. We might destroy some evidence."

He gestured toward Vledder.

"Go downstairs and use the radio to get ahold of the desk sergeant at headquarters. No wait, better use a phone booth. Everybody listens to the police band these days, and I don't want the press here. Not yet, anyway. Ask the sergeant to alert the guys from forensics, the lab, and so on. Also ask for a plumber."

"A plumber?"

"Yes, a person with tools able to open and close pipes, remove gratings, fix leaks, you know."

Astonished, Vledder looked at his mentor.

"What in the world do you want with a plumber?"

"What do you think? I want to solve the case, of course. Why else are we here?" He raised a cautioning finger. "And don't forget the dactyloscopic service. I'm very curious to see what sort of fingerprints we can find here. You see, this is an interesting apartment."

Vledder's face looked disappointed.

"Listen, DeKok," he said, darkly, "I know that you're very good, an old hand. And I'm still young and I can still learn a lot from you. I get that." His tone changed, became almost threatening. "But I've had it with the hide-and-seek games. You tell me now how you knew about this apartment or I won't move another muscle."

"Oh, really?" DeKok rubbed his chin.

"Yes!" It sounded like a challenge.

DeKok made a sad, almost comical gesture.

"Well, if you put it that way..." For another instant he kept his face expressionless and then it changed into a warm, broad smile. "You're right. You most certainly are entitled to a complete explanation. I just wanted to stimulate your imagination, that's all. That's why I was so mysterious. Believe me, it isn't mysterious at all. It's no more than following up on a certain train of thought.

I'll explain it as soon as you've finished calling. Fair enough?"

"All right."

DeKok took another tour of the apartment as soon as Vledder had disappeared. In the foyer, on a peg behind the door, he found a blue plastic raincoat. On a shelf above was a dark handbag. He took the purse to the living room and inspected the contents. It contained the usual makeup articles—handkerchief, lipstick, mirror, powder puff. There was also a Dutch passport in the name of Nanette Bogaard. Searching a bit further he found a small flashlight, a key ring with keys, and a small, flat cardboard box filled with glass ampoules of morphine.

Vledder came back within a few minutes.

"Well?"

Vledder sighed.

"It isn't going to be easy, but the 'thundering herd' will be here shortly." He threw himself down next to DeKok on the couch.

DeKok smiled. Everybody knew his special name for the horde of specialists who always responded to murder crime scenes. Vledder's remarks meant the full crew would be here—photographers, fingerprint people, forensic experts. This was the complete crew, not just a weekend standby group.

"Excellent," said DeKok, "very good. Meanwhile I found something special here."

He showed the raincoat and the handbag with passport and ampoules. Vledder scrutinized the items.

"Well, at least we can be sure of one thing," he said after a while. "Nanette was here in this apartment."

DeKok nodded.

"But she left in the nude."

"Is this," Vledder asked, "a conclusion based solely on your observation of her clothes and the personal effects we found here? Or is this also a part of a particular train of thought?"

DeKok smiled.

"Both," he answered. "When we found Nanette's body parts in the dump, I was puzzled. Why those horrible mutilations, why was the body cut into pieces? I just couldn't find a reasonable explanation. Mutilations after death are certainly nothing new, but the thing is that they usually serve some sort of purpose. However twisted and criminal, there is typically a reason. Just think about Kameda, the Japanese suitcase murder of a few years back. We found just the torso and the arms in the suitcase. The head, the legs, and the hands were missing. We concluded the killer wanted to make it more difficult to identify the victim. As you know, the head and hands provide practically the only sure means of identifying people. Humans don't have brands, or logos, except for body art. With just a torso it is almost impossible to identify the remains with any degree of confidence. Conversely, the head offers all sorts of methods for positive identification. Just think about the eyes, the mouth, the hair, the shape of the nose, the teeth. Hands, too, are characteristic because of the fingers and fingerprints."

DeKok was now in full "orator mode."

"In addition to obscuring the identity of the victim," he continued animatedly, "criminals sometimes use mutilation to dispose of the corpse. We have numerous examples in the history of crime. I name, just by way of example, the infamous French killer Landru, who first strangled his victims and then burned them. Without amputations, his method of disposal would have been impossible. His coal-burning stove was not very big."

"A nice man, this Mr. Landru," laughed Vledder.

"Indeed, but I digress. We're not dealing with the Case Landru, but with the Case Nanette. What struck me as incongruous was finding all of them. There was nothing missing—head, torso, hands were all there. It seemed significant to find them relatively close together. One could only conclude the mutilations had not been performed in order to hide the identity of the victim."

Vledder moved a little deeper into the cushions of the sofa, intently serving as DeKok's audience.

"But what was the purpose? It remained a puzzle. It was a worker at the dump, Claus Boer, who told me the garbage in which the remains were found came from Amsterdam West. Even so I didn't make the connection. It caused me a few extra grey hairs, I can tell you, trying to figure out the killer's purpose." He smiled. "Remember how the suburbs there became absorbed by the city and new developments? Most of the apartment developments formed small villages. They had names like Ditch Canal, Mill Lake, Ox Village, Halfway, and so on. To make it harder, or easier, depending on your point of view, some of the original names were replaced with new ones. Even individual buildings had names. In Mill Lake and Ox Village they continued building residential barracks with assembly line methods. Anyway, all these new buildings are equipped with individual garbage chutes covered with airtight flaps in the kitchens. Residents pop any sort of refuse into the chutes. Large containers below the building catch and gather everything. Then the trucks from sanitation pick up the containers, gather the contents, and away we go."

"I understand," exclaimed Vledder, "of course, the chute! The murderer got rid of the corpse by means of the chute, and that naturally could only have been done in pieces. The chutes aren't all that big."

"Indeed," nodded DeKok. "In the case of a heavyset person it would have been impossible: the parts would have had to be smaller yet. But Nanette was a slight girl, not very big at all."

He became silent, lost in thought. It was as if he saw it happen. He could envision detailed images in a fleeting flashback. Only after several minutes did he continue.

"Of course, there remained questions. How could we establish which building, which flat, which chute? In short, exactly where was Nanette Bogaard killed?" He pulled his lower lip over his upper lip. "I took those questions to the inestimable Mr. Slosser of the registrar's office. As a point of departure I used the names of people we have met and about whom we knew something. The question was whether any of those names could be connected with an apartment building in Amsterdam West."

He used his pinky to rub the bridge of his nose.

"At first it seemed hopeless," he went on. "The name Laurens, in all possible spellings, offered no connection. I'd put the brother at the top of my list because of his supposed anatomical knowledge. But because we don't know if Laurens is a first name or a surname, I couldn't make a connection. Nanette apparently never registered in Amsterdam before she lived over Ye Three Roses. It occurred to me Brother Laurens might also not be registered in the city. It also seemed to me Nanette must have met him in her capacity as a nurse, before her arrival in Amsterdam."

"Excellent," admired Vledder, "really excellent." Neither he nor DeKok noted his use of one of DeKok's favorite phrases.

"Barry Wielen," continued DeKok, ignoring the interruption, "appeared to be a bit of a butterfly. He had lived at a number of addresses in Amsterdam, but never in Amsterdam West. I was beginning to think we would be wasting an entire Sunday in the files, all for nothing. Suddenly old man Slosser discovered the elder Staaten wasn't registered at Emperor's Canal at all; his address was recorded as Wood's Edge 123."

Startled, Vledder looked up.

"This flat?" he said.

DeKok nodded.

"I almost couldn't believe it myself—it precipitated my theatrics with the doll. When I picked that old thing up at the dump, I really had no ulterior motive. It was more a whim, a sentimental impulse from an old man. Somehow, somewhere, I saw a connection between the old, discarded doll and the young girl who had been so brutally murdered. Only later did I realize the doll had probably been found in the same area as the body parts. Maybe it seemed a long shot, but the doll and the remains of Nanette *could* have been dumped by the same truck."

"I understand. So when that little boy and the woman both recognized Bibette, you felt Nanette's remains came from this building as well."

"That's so," nodded DeKok.

"So, old man Staaten killed Nanette after all."

DeKok rubbed his hand over his face.

"I, eh, I don't think so."

"What!?"

"I don't think Staaten killed Nanette."

Totally confused, Vledder looked at his mentor.

"But this is *his* apartment! He's registered at this address."

"Registered, yes. But that doesn't necessarily mean he lives here. The elder Staaten is a man with refined taste, a connoisseur. He loves atmosphere, coziness, intimacy. He surrounds himself with beautiful things—paintings, handsome and comfortable furniture. Just look around you. This is a sparsely furnished apartment without sphere or personality, tastelessly decorated. It's more like a hotel room. No surroundings for the elder Staaten. He would—"

Suddenly DeKok stopped talking.

"What's the matter?" whispered Vledder.

"Listen, somebody is at the door."

"The herd?"

"Too soon, no, they can't be…"

They rose as one and inched toward the foyer door. They could clearly hear the front door being opened. Seconds later they stood nose to nose with a man. It was Vledder's fault. He opened the living room door a little too soon.

As soon as the man spotted the detectives he reacted immediately. In a flash he turned and ran from the flat.

"The beard!" yelled DeKok. "The beard from The Red Lion. Catch him!"

Vledder started after the man.

20

The bearded man ran along the gallery. His long legs moved at incredible speed, despite a floppy pair of pants. The pale, loose jacket flapped like the wings of a bat. He did not look around.

Vledder followed with a savage determination. He was furious with himself for his actions back in the apartment. He had given the game away prematurely. He had been too ambitious, greedy. He'd given the man just enough time to make his escape. They ran on.

The sudden exertion made Vledder pant heavily. He felt his heart thump in his chest like a steam hammer. The man with the beard fled before him. The distance between him and his quarry increased steadily.

The man shot into the elevator lobby at the end of the gallery. He realized in a flash it would be madness to wait for an elevator. He sprinted to the top of the stairs.

As he passed the bank of elevators on the floor below, he aimed for the next set of stairs. An elevator door opened. A few women and children emerged. Unaware of the situation, the small group formed a sudden obstacle for the bearded man. They were too close. He could not avoid them. His speed was too great.

Right in front of him was a little girl, perhaps six

years old or less, with a doll in her arms. He jumped wildly in a desperate attempt to avoid the child. It was an uncalculated jump and he lost control. His left foot slipped, found no traction. He fell on the granite floor with a sickening thud.

Dazed, almost unconscious, he remained down. He heard the screams of women and children from what seemed a distance. It was a strangely thrilling sound of people in panic. He opened his eyes and looked for the source. He could not see very well. The images blurred. Next to his head was a doll. He could make out the shape and the features. It was an old plastic doll with a fixed smile. It fascinated him. He did not know why. He could not tear his eyes away from that fixed, soulless smile. He was still looking at it when he lost consciousness.

"What was the verdict at the hospital?"

Vledder sighed.

"He's in shock. For the time being we're not allowed to ask him any questions."

"Is his condition serious?"

"No, not exactly. The doctor thinks he will be all right in a few days. In retrospect it wasn't all that bad."

"Is the little girl injured?"

"Nothing but a few scrapes and bruises on her arms and legs. Her mother already took her home."

"I'm glad for that," said DeKok, relieved.

Vledder bit on his lower lip.

"Me too, believe me. I really feel partly responsible for that tumble, you know. I should never have given Pierre a chance to run away. If I had just let him enter all the way, we would have had him. That guy was so fast."

"I hope," grinned DeKok, "you arranged for surveillance in the hospital."

"Of course, what do you think? I managed to convince the commissaris to assign two constables. One in the corridor and the other one next to the bed."

"What about the windows?"

Vledder shook his head wearily.

"No problem. The windows look out on a closed courtyard; he cannot escape."

DeKok rose from his chair.

"Excellent," he said. "Really excellent. Two constables seem more than enough then. I wouldn't want to lose our friend at this late date, you see."

"For certain, you worked hard enough to get ahold of him. Have you heard anything from technical services?"

Slowly DeKok nodded.

"Yes, just before you came back from the hospital, I talked with Doctor Beskes from the lab. He told me that they'd found blonde hair on the sides of the garbage chute and in the grating of the drainpipe in the shower. They also found evidence of human tissue, corroborating my theory that Nanette was killed and dismembered inside the flat."

"And what about prints?" asked Vledder while nodding agreement with DeKok's statement.

"They found prints all over the place—in the kitchen, the bathroom, everywhere. With so many, it's too soon to identify individual prints. They have to be compared and correlated."

"What do you think?"

"I think they'll find matches."

Vledder looked at him probingly.

"You mean, eh, the prints will probably belong to Pierre Popko and Nanette?"

"Yes."

Vledder shook his head and sighed.

"To be completely honest, I don't understand a thing. How, for instance, did those two get to use the apartment belonging to Staaten? And why would Popko murder Nanette? What motive did he have? I can't see it. Really, I can't see it."

With hands deeply buried in his pockets, DeKok began to pace up and down the large detective room. Slowly his feet shuffled over the worn linoleum. Despite his success so far, he was depressed and discouraged.

He halted in front of the window. The rain hid the rooftops across the street in a nebulous veil.

"Raining cats and dogs," he murmured. "Dog days."

Suddenly he thought about his old mother and her superstitious fear of those days in July. It evoked tender feelings. DeKok smiled softly to himself. He saw the so-familiar face in his mind's eye, two sparkling eyes in a lovely face full of dear wrinkles. "Careful, my boy," he heard her say, "the dog days of summer can be dangerous...dangerous...danger..." Her voice echoed in his brain.

He remained motionless in front of the window for a while longer, trying to come to a decision. Then he turned, took his hat and coat, and waddled out of the office.

"Come," he called from the door, "we're going to the hospital. I want that painter's story today, now!"

Vledder looked at him in astonishment.

"But," he called after him, "what about the doctor?"

DeKok ignored him. Unperturbed, he walked on. Vledder followed him, shaking his head, his raincoat in a bunch on his shoulders.

DeKok could never really get used to the typical smell of a hospital—that combination of Lysol, carbolic soap, and other, less identifiable odors. Whenever he had to visit a hospital in the line of duty, he made his stay as short as possible.

"Where is he?" he nudged Vledder.

"Upstairs, second floor."

They climbed the stairs. A couple of young nurses darted past them. Vledder showed his most pleasant face and a beaming smile. DeKok did not exert himself.

They found a young constable in the corridor on the second floor. He stood in front of a door, legs wide apart.

DeKok grinned at him in a friendly sort of way.

"I'm Inspector DeKok."

"Yessir, with a kay-oh-kay. I've seen you before," laughed the constable.

"Excellent. Where's your partner?"

"Inside. Holding the suspect's hand, I expect."

"Excellent," repeated DeKok grinning, "just fine. Just call him out here, will you? Vledder and I will take over for a while. Look around, get a cup of coffee, pinch the nurse, whatever. Be back here in about half an hour."

"Half an hour?" grimaced the constable.

"Yes, about that. And don't worry about him in the meantime. We'll take good care of him, and we won't leave before you're back."

The young constable nodded. He opened the door of the room and motioned for his partner to come outside. The partner, a big, dark, muscular man, was sitting next to the bed, a bit embarrassed.

"Come, Sister of Mercy," he joked, "the detectives will take over for a while."

His partner rose from the chair gratefully. Any interruption in the boredom of the assignment was welcome. His large face beaming, he left the room.

As soon as the constables had left, Vledder and DeKok approached the bed. They stood and looked at the man who had surprised them in the apartment. They renewed the confrontation.

Pierre Popko looked pale. He was on his back. Bandages formed a sort of turban around his head. He looked calmly at his visitors. The blue eyes were clear.

DeKok took his old felt hat from his head, keeping it in front of his chest. It was an uncomfortable, awkward gesture, as if he did not really know what to do with it.

Vledder looked at him from the side. DeKok irritated him at such moments. Forced bashfulness on his mentor's part exasperated him to no end. It was nothing but a posture. Vledder knew that. It was designed to keep an opponent off guard. It was so evident, transparent. Vledder could simply not understand how anybody could be fooled.

"How are you?" he heard him ask. It sounded worried.

Pierre Popko gave a wan smile.

"Not too bad, yes, not too bad." Carefully he felt for the bandages on his head. "My head still hurts."

DeKok pushed a chair closer to the head end of the bed and sat down.

"Well, that was quite a fall you took."

The painter tried to grin.

"Yes," he said with a grimace, "you might say that. How, eh, how's the child?"

"All right. She had a few scrapes and bruises, nothing serious. She's home already."

"I tried to avoid her." The hand on the white sheet made a helpless movement. "But I couldn't. I was going rather fast, and the descent of the stairs increased my speed too much. I was too close, too fast."

Silence fell over the room.

Vledder walked away from the foot of the bed. He went to the window and sat down on a short bench, took out his notebook, and poised himself to take notes. He knew this was just the preliminary skirmish. Before long, DeKok would steer the conversation in the direction of the murder. He knew his mentor so well. That was part of his tactic. He would approach the subject in which he was interested calmly, obliquely. It was a sideways approach, virtually undetectable. The painter turned his head carefully; it was obviously painful for him to do so.

"You're Inspector DeKok, aren't you?"

"You know me?" asked DeKok, nodding agreement.

"Kristel told me," answered the painter after a slight hesitation.

"You know Kristel?"

"Kristel is an old friend," smiled the painter.

"You've known her for years?"

"As a friend, yes. I've known her since before she started Ye Three Roses on Duke Street. I met her through her brother."

"Frank Bogaard?"

"Yes indeed, that's what he calls himself. For one reason or another he assumed his mother's name as a pen name. His real name is Frank van Daalen. Frank wrote a number of interesting books. I like his work. Somebody introduced us one evening in a bar. It was the beginning of a short friendship."

"What happened to him?"

Pierre Popko made a slight, almost imperceptible movement with his shoulders.

"I don't know. As I said, our friendship didn't last long. He hung around with people I didn't care for. It eventually resulted in a rift. Later I heard he might have been hooked on drugs. I don't know whether it's true or not. We lost touch."

DeKok nodded.

"But, eh, your friendship with Kristel survived?"

Popko showed some discomfort for the first time since they had entered. The question seemed to worry him.

"Well?" pressed DeKok.

"My, eh, my friendship with Kristel survived."

His voice sounded suddenly sharper.

The detective leaned closer.

"And when Nanette disappeared…" As casually as possible he posed the question. Like a hawk he looked for a reaction.

A slight blush colored the face of the painter.

"That…that's something else. It had nothing to do with Kristel and me. I mean, it was outside our friendship. Kristel understood that."

"I don't." DeKok shook his head.

"What?"

"I don't understand it."

Pierre Popko sighed deeply.

"Nanette, Nanette was like a drug. Perhaps in retrospect I should call the relationship a disease, an aberration." He spread his arms wide. "She loved me, she said. She loved only me."

He shook his head and closed his eyes tightly. His body shook. His lips trembled above his beard. His hands crumpled the sheets.

"She was a snake, a viper," he hissed. "Believe me, the past few days have been hell." He sighed, overcome with emotion. It sounded like a sob. "But I have been cleansed, cleansed…"

DeKok felt the painter's face with the back of his hand. The face was hot. He feared a renewed shock. After all, this interrogation had been prohibited by the attending physician. Without permission, if something happened…

"Let's discuss this calmly," he said softly, soothingly. "Calmly like reasonable people. It'll do you good, believe me. Clearing the air will come as a relief. You *do* want to talk about it, don't you?"

Pierre nodded weakly.

DeKok took the sheet and used a tip to carefully wipe the man's sharp nose, the corners of his eyes, and his cheeks. The painter's face was bathed in sweat. Drops of sweat beaded on his beard.

"When you visited your old friend Kristel at Ye Three Roses, is that when you first met Nanette?"

"Yes."

"You found her attractive?"

"Yes."

"You fell in love?"

"Not immediately."

DeKok paused. He smiled encouragingly at the painter. Pierre had become a lot calmer. The friendly, softly insistent voice of DeKok had calmed him. He did not shake anymore.

"What happened next?"

"Nanette was so different from Kristel, more outgoing, more frivolous. When she found out I painted, she forced herself on me persistently, shamelessly. She wanted to come to the studio to model for me."

Softly he grinned to himself.

"At first I refused. Really, I didn't want to get involved. You see, she was downright scary. Whenever she was with me I felt confused, unsure of myself, restless. It was as if I didn't exist anymore. You understand? I lost track of who I was. I became a creature without a will of my own."

He remained silent for a while.

"One night Nanette told me she loved me."

He covered his face with both hands.

"From then on everything went wrong."

"How's that?"

Popko licked his dry lips.

"She told me that she would make me famous, a great painter. She believed painting was more than a matter of talent or technique; it was more a matter of marketability. It didn't matter so much what you painted, as long as people talked about it. She told me she knew a reporter. She was certain she could convince him to write a number of articles about me."

He smiled wanly and swallowed before he continued.

"It sounded too good to be true. You must keep in mind I'd never been very successful with my paintings. I live in poverty, really, in an old barn on Prince's Island. I call it my studio, but it's little more than a shack. At night it is a playground for rats. Once, when I showed Staaten how the rats had been gnawing on my paints, he gave me the key to his flat in Wood's Edge. I was allowed to use the flat as a bedroom."

He rubbed the back of his hands over his dry lips.

"I used to take Nanette there from time to time. Whenever she was with me, I lived in a sort of dream. It was almost a drunken stupor. I felt like I walked on air, wings on both feet."

DeKok nodded, understanding.

"How did Nanette meet Staaten?"

"Through me. I told her about Staaten, told her the apartment belonged to him. I explained that he was wealthy and owned a fantastic collection of paintings. I told her he sometimes gave me a commission."

He took a deep breath. Talking seemed to become easier.

"She pressed me," he continued, "to introduce her to him. She wanted to meet him, ostensibly to persuade Staaten to give me important projects."

"And that's how you received the commission for the nude on the sofa?"

"That painting was not a commission." He shook his head.

"What?"

"No, it was just another of Nanette's ideas. 'Let's show old man Staaten what I look like,' she said. 'The more he sees, the more curious he'll be.'"

"Why use the red sofa?"

"That was another of her ideas. Once, in a sentimental mood, Staaten had told her about his wife. Nanette was a good listener when she wanted to be. She knew the red sofa was a favorite of the late Mrs. Staaten."

Pierre Popko swallowed.

"She wanted to get old Staaten crazy enough that he would ask her to marry him."

"And she enlisted you to help her?"

"Yes. I made a few nice sketches of her. Pretty realistic, almost provocative. I showed them to Staaten. He was visibly shaken."

"How could you help her? She loved you, or so she said. And you were supposed to help her trap Staaten? That's incomprehensible."

Pierre buried his face in his hands again.

"I don't know. I don't know anymore." There was despair in his voice. "She talked about a marriage of convenience. It wouldn't mean anything, wouldn't affect our relationship. On the contrary, it would bind us closer together. A marriage with a rich man would also afford her the opportunity to do a lot for me professionally. And as soon as Staaten died, there would be plenty of years left."

He moved his head from side to side.

"I really don't know anymore. I was simply drugged, mesmerized. I was also apathetic. It was as if I had lost every shred of judgment."

"When did you regain your senses?" asked DeKok, watching him closely.

Popko pressed himself into a sitting position. He sat straight up in bed and bent his head backward. His mouth was partially open. It was as if he was stretching himself after a long and deep sleep.

"I finally woke up," he said softly, "when I saw her dead in front of me. It was as if I had been awakened from a nightmare. It was all so unreal, even her death. When I finally realized it wasn't a nightmare, I cried over her corpse. I wept a long time, so long I had no tears left."

"And then?"

The painter slid back down in the bed. He rested his head on the pillow and stared at the ceiling.

"Suddenly," he went on, "I realized Nanette had to disappear. She couldn't remain in the apartment. That was impossible...unthinkable. After all, Staaten knew I used the flat. I panicked. In a wild, unthinking impulse I lifted her onto my shoulder and walked out onto the gallery. There's an emergency staircase. Almost nobody ever uses it."

He paused again, lost in memories.

"I was almost downstairs when a car stopped at the bottom and somebody came up the stairs. My heart stopped, I can tell you. I turned around and climbed the stairs as rapidly as possible. It was easy. Nanette wasn't heavy. I saw a number of cars and bicycles on the road behind the building. Suddenly I realized I was visible from everywhere. Anybody could notice me. Scared, I ran with the corpse over my shoulder as fast as I could, but my fear grew more intense. I heard sounds that weren't there. I saw doors open that were closed. It was hell, complete hell. I think I'd lost my mind when I finally got her back in the flat."

The painter stopped talking, rubbed his hands over his face, his beard. Sweat poured out of him.

"On the sofa, on the sofa in the living room I thought about a way to get rid of her."

"That's when you thought about the garbage chute?"

He nodded slowly in reply.

"A strange calm came over me. I was resigned. Never before in my life do I remember ever having been that calm. I undressed her carefully. When she was naked, I carried her to the bathroom and lowered her into the shower stall."

"That's where it happened?"

"Yes, that's where it happened," he answered with a sigh.

DeKok fell back against the support of the chair. He felt torpid. The interrogation of the painter had sucked the air out of him.

He thought about the conversation, allowing every word to pass in review. He had an uncanny knack for total recall. It was as if a tape recorder played back the entire conversation. He reexamined every word, intonation, and expression in detail. He checked to be certain he had everything. Was it sufficient to satisfy the district attorney, the judge advocate, the courts? He even considered the defense's potential reaction.

He looked at his watch. More than half an hour had passed. The constables had not yet returned. He wondered idly where they had gone.

Suddenly he remembered something vital. There was one question he had not yet asked. He looked at the painter.

"But what was the motive? I mean, what was the immediate cause that triggered you to kill her?"

Popko's eyes opened wide. His face showed nothing but utter amazement.

"Kill her?"

"Yes."

"But I just got rid of the body. I didn't kill her."

"What!?"

"I didn't kill her. Nanette was already dead when I found her."

DeKok swallowed in total astonishment. Never before in his long career had an answer shocked him so. It was as if the room started to spin around him. The floor was disappearing underneath his chair. He pressed his eyes closed to shut himself off from the turmoil. From a distance he heard Vledder move.

The door of the room opened. Both constables were visible in the opening.

"Sorry," said the younger of the two, "it took a little longer than expected. When we finally found the kitchen, the coffee wasn't ready."

DeKok rose weakly.

"Never mind," he said groggily.

He picked up his felt hat from the bed, murmured a hasty farewell, and shuffled into the corridor.

Vledder looked after him from the door opening. His face was serious, not to say distraught. He felt instinctively it would be better not to follow his partner, not this time. Vledder would have to step back and let DeKok take the next step by himself. It became his mission, his duty.

The belt had been twisted so often that it resembled a rope. DeKok pulled it a little tighter around his old raincoat and pressed his fists deeper into the pockets. Slowly he strolled away from the hospital across a number of bridges, along canals, oblivious to his surroundings. A surly, gruff look clouded his face. Every once in a while he used a handkerchief to wipe the rain from his face. It did not slow him down. In his typical rolling gait he walked on, past the ferries, across the Dam. There were times when he hated his profession, when he would rather be anything else except a detective. At those times he hated the law, hated the justice system. This was one of those moments.

He walked the length of a number of streets and then turned the corner of Duke Street. In front of Ye Three Roses he halted and looked up at the old cast-iron sign over the door. It was decorated with a shield, a coat of arms. He noticed it for the first time. Three red roses on a white field.

He looked at it for a long time, contemplated leaving. But he knew that would be useless, senseless.

He placed a finger on the buzzer and pushed.

21

Vledder had not forgotten the invitation from his mentor, partner, and friend. A week later on a Sunday, he and Celine had come visiting. Mrs. DeKok had, as promised, made a special effort to make it a festive occasion. A small, intimate party. Later that evening they were comfortably gathered in the living room.

Celine was a darling of a girl, that is, *a young woman*, DeKok corrected himself in silence. He admired the good sense and taste of his pupil. At first Celine had been a bit withdrawn, shy. Eventually she participated cheerfully in the conversation.

When there was a gap in the conversation, Celine said unexpectedly, "So, did Kristel van Daalen kill Nanette?"

"Why the sudden interest?" asked DeKok, perplexed.

She laughed, a bit shyly.

"I lived through that time with you, in a sense. When we were together, I helped Dick think. Didn't I, Dick?"

Vledder grinned, a bit embarrassed.

"Yes," he swallowed, "she helped me think."

"Well, what was the result?"

She smiled a sunny smile.

"I would never have thought of Kristel. Actually, she was the one I least suspected."

The grey sleuth pushed his lower lip forward.

"Did Dick tell you everything? How we surprised Brother Laurens at the funeral? How we arrested him? How—"

"Yes," interrupted Celine, "I know all that, but you dealt with Kristel on your own."

DeKok sighed.

"Kristel, yes…"

He paused to order his thoughts.

"After Pierre Popko," he began hesitatingly, "told me in the hospital he hadn't killed Nanette but had found her already dead, I suddenly realized the true chain of events. Kristel was responsible for Nanette's death. To clinch the case, her fingerprints were found in the flat later by the experts."

He took a sip from his cognac.

"Kristel," he continued, "knew about the flat in Wood's Edge. She had known for some time. She and Pierre met there, long before Nanette came to spoil the idyll. Just like Nanette, she had a key to the apartment. That Thursday, just after Nanette left, Pierre stopped by Ye Three Roses to tell Nanette that he would be at the flat a little later than usual. He was working on something in his studio and he wanted to finish it. He asked Kristel to pass the message to Nanette. Kristel promised to do so. She didn't tell him Nanette had already left. It seemed like a unique opportunity. She closed up shop, then went to the apartment. She used her key to enter. After a short but intense exchange of words, she strangled Nanette. Kristel has strong hands. She's been playing tennis for years, at least three to four times a week."

"But why?" asked Celine, making an impatient gesture.

DeKok sighed a deep sigh and took another sip from his drink.

"Well, you see, despite everything, I feel a deep sympathy for Kristel. And it's not just because she is an extremely beautiful woman. Kristel loved Pierre Popko. She had been in love with him for a long time. When Nanette appeared, she relinquished her love. She reluctantly let go of her lover. It was a constant source of sorrow and regret. But she couldn't fight Nanette. Nanette had an almost hypnotic influence over men. She could have any man she wanted, just by snapping her fingers. Kristel could only hope Pierre would get over his infatuation. She must have held on to the hope he would wake up and come back to her."

They listened to him with bated breath. After a short hesitation, he went on.

"When Nanette revealed her plans to marry Staaten, Pierre lost his head. He confided in Kristel and told her about Nanette's plans and aspirations. Kristel was furious. More than anything else this was so contrary to her own sense of morality, so she called Nanette to account." He remained silent for a moment. "That's when Nanette threatened her."

Celine looked at DeKok with wide eyes. "Nanette threatened her?"

"Yes, Nanette threatened Kristel. It became her death sentence. If Kristel were to interfere in any way at all, if she so much as tried to stop her, Nanette said she would get Pierre hooked on drugs. She would turn Pierre into a vegetable, just as she had Frank."

"Morphine!" panted Celine.

"Yes, morphine."

Celine's eyes flashed in anger.

"What a snake," she hissed. A blush of complete indignation colored her cheeks.

DeKok smiled sadly.

"Yes," he said, "a snake in the shape of an angel."